Belisama

Alan Richard

Grosvenor House
Publishing Limited

This book is published by
Grosvenor House Publishing Ltd
Link House
140 The Broadway, Tolworth, Surrey, KT6 7HT.
www.grosvenorhousepublishing.co.uk

This book is a work of fiction. Any resemblance to
people or events, past or present, is purely coincidental.

A CIP record for this book
is available from the British Library

Paperback ISBN 978-1-83615-412-9
eBook ISBN 978-1-83615-529-4

For Philippa:
partner, wife, soulmate,
and love of my life.

Belisama Introduction

Belisama (modern day River Ribble) is a Historical Fiction novel centred around the Roman fort and settlement of Bremetennacum (modern day Ribchester, England). All the events take place during one lunar cycle in the spring of 122 CE. Readers should note that this is not a slow burn coming-of-age novel. Roman girls and boys grew up fast in Roman times with girls expected to behave as grown women at thirteen years of age, and boys as grown men at fourteen. According to most sources, twenty-five to thirty-three years of life expectancy was common, although there were some exceptions.

While we may well look back in horror at the deprivations and cruelties of times gone by, the novel is concerned with life as it probably was and how ordinary people lived and died through extraordinary times and circumstances on the troubled island of Britannia. Emperor Hadrian wanted to establish defined borders and bring an era of peace, culture, and stability across the Empire, but I speculate that many in northern Britannia boiled with resentment at life under Roman rule, even as the tribes in the south had moved on from the Boudica rebellion and bought into the Roman way of life.

I wish to acknowledge the Roman Museum at Ribchester, which gave me the inspiration to author the novel, although in no way is that to be construed as an endorsement of the novel. Also, I acknowledge all the academics for the historical literature who's works and translations have revealed some of what was a vast ancient Empire that still fascinates many to this day.

Roman Names and Modern-Day Equivalents

Roman	Modern-Day
Arbus Fluvius	Humber
Arma Officinas (Official Armoury)	Walton-le-Dale
Belisama	River Ribble
Bremetennacum	Ribchester
Caerleon	Newport, South Wales
Calunium	Lancaster
Coccium	Wigan
Dacia	Romania
Deva	Chester
Eboracum	York
Londinium	London
Lonsdale	Lune Valley
Luguvalium	Carlisle
Luna	River Lune
Mamucium	Manchester
Portus Piscium (Speculative) Hill Fort (Speculative)	Freckleton Pool and Kirkham, respectively.
Stanegate Road	Frontier road running from Carlisle to Corbridge
Trough Valley (Speculative)	Trough of Bowland

Contents

Chapter One

River Pilot

(Fluvius Gabanator)

Regulus was hopeless first thing in the morning, and the morning of 21st March 122 CE made no difference to that indisputable cast iron fact. He blundered and fumbled from his bed like he had spent all night in one of the village taverns at Bremetennacum and flopped into one of the chairs by the fireplace.

He gazed, bleary eyed, at his mother, Seren, as she carried on sewing by dim candlelight, unperturbed by the usual morning performance of her tall gangly fourteen-year-old son. Patient about her craft, her long brown hair draped down across her face as she continued her work one push and pull of the thread at a time. Regulus marvelled at her stoic industriousness and how she managed to be awake so early.

There was only the two of them in the small two roomed ground floor apartment. Boxes of material, clothes, strips of leather, and buckles surrounded Seren ready for sewing, repairing, completing ready for market day and collection by her customers. A black iron pot hung over the embers in the fireplace and puffs of steam rose from the breakfast porridge. A small wooden table, stood against the wall under the window, began to appear from the shadows as the first light of

1

dawn crept into the room. Seren stood, served two wooden bowls of porridge from the black iron pot, and handed one to Regulus.

"You'd better have something to eat," she said.

They both ate with gratitude, mindful of the deliciousness of hot food after such a harsh winter and the scarcity that had come with it. At least the first warmer days of spring, and the promise of better times ahead, brought some relief. They had survived; some had not. Life and death balanced on a high wire with no care for status or wealth, and although extra money was always welcome, Seren's careful budgeting had got them both through.

"This river trip should only take a couple of days," said Regulus as he finished his food and prepared to leave.

"You will be careful, won't you?" asked Seren.

Regulus gave her a youthful carefree grin.

"Always!".

She looked at him with her kind grey eyes, knowing how cavalier and carefree he could be, which clashed with her careful and methodical approach to life. She sometimes wondered how he had managed to stay in one piece. She went back to her work, head bowed, nimble fingers stitching a leather strap around a buckle to finish off a belt. Days were long and work was hard, but the money from sales at market, clothing repairs for villagers, and Regulus's modest Cadet River Pilot stipend paid the rent and put food on the table.

She allowed herself a sigh.

"At least we have that," she whispered to herself.

Regulus grabbed his small leather bag of meagre possessions, knife in his tunic belt and rushed out onto the Roman road, which teemed with life even at this early hour. Market stalls were set, bakers had been baking, butchers chopping, and the relentless clanking of the blacksmith's hammer at the forge echoed around the houses. Children ran around chasing each other and delighted in teasing the cantankerous old baker. As the children chased each other, a hissing gaggle of geese chased the children and flustered hens clucked about trying to stay out of the way.

The gentle green slopes of the north and south sides of the Belisama valley ran down to the river, and a grey gravel Roman road cut a straight line from the top of one side to the other. At the bottom of the valley on the north side of the river, a civilian settlement had sprung up on the east and west side of the road. Just before a wooden bridge, a Roman fort straddled the road with a north and south gate, home to five hundred Asturian Cavalry veterans. The fort was called Bremetennacum, but most called it "Bremetenn" for short. A symbol of Roman rule and power, not one amphorae of olive oil crossed the Belisama without permission and authorisation.

Regulus walked down the road and into the fort. Four gates, north, south, east, and west with a square in the middle, and wooden barracks for the soldiers filled most of the area. One of the soldiers waved him through as he walked past and out to the river on the other side. He could see the mast of the *Belisama Cygnus* poking up from below the top of the riverbank by the fort. He knew he must be onboard before "Gabo", the River Pilot, to complete all the necessary checks, and be ready for the voyage down to the Belisama estuary. They were bound for the fish port, the so-called Portus Piscium home to some of the Setantii, the coastal tribe of the marshes.

As the loading dock came into view, he could see the ten slave rowers loading the long narrow and shallow boat with all the cargo for trading at the Portus Piscium. An officious little man sat on a tiny stool scribbling notes for the manifest on top of a cashbox, which served as a makeshift desk. Cargo was being loaded and secured: amphorae of olive oil and wine imported from the south of the Empire, venison, sacks of bread loaves, early spring root vegetables grown in the fertile fields of the Belisama valley, and barrels of salted pork.

The Setantii had grown to enjoy the trappings and varied diet of Roman rule. They were happy to exchange the flounder, shrimp, eel, and prized salmon for bread and wine – especially the wine. They had become experts in making the fish sauce that Romans loved so much. Even the Romanised Brigante in the village had grown to love it. All, it appeared, except Regulus. He hated the stuff. To him, it smelled and tasted like rotten fish. He was sure there must be others in the vastness of the Roman Empire who shared his opinion, but he had yet to meet one.

Towering over the whole scene and supervising the work was First Spear Centurion Decimus, the Primus Pilus. Six feet tall, he stood bolt to attention in full uniform. His stern and battle-scarred face was expressionless, yet his sharp brown eyes missed nothing. He would bark in a thunderous militaristic voice at anyone out of order, or a sack out of place during the loading process. Although he was a veteran of the twentieth legion, the famous Legio XX, and forty-five years of age, he was as fit and muscular as men half his years. He had been seconded to Bremetenn to represent the legion fifteen years ago, and, having won the respect and admiration of the veterans, the Prefect of the fort had requested that he stay.

Regulus walked down the steps and onto the loading dock.

"Good morning, Primus Pilus Decimus, how goes your day?"

"Well enough Cadet Fluvius Gabanator," he replied, his voice and language strictly formal. He growled something at the man on the stool about finishing the accounts and manifest. The man's beady eyes scrutinised everything one last time and he locked the box ready for loading.

"Everything is in order Primus Pilus Decimus."

"Very good, Clerk of the Fort, see to it that the cashbox, accounts, and manifest are handed over to Fluvius Gabanator before departure," said Decimus as he took two steps back, stamped his right foot, and stood to attention.

A short stocky man with a confident air breezed down the steps to the loading dock. He had a head full of slicked back black hair, and a black, neatly trimmed beard. He beamed with approval at the scene before him. His arms were full of scrolls: charts, moon and tide dates and times, and other writings about the Belisama and the marshes he had gathered over the years. He noted his cadet checking the ropes and sail rigging, oiling the pulleys and he muttered to himself that all was in order. Fluvius Gabanator, was his formal title, but everyone called him "Gabo", his formal title being such a mouthful. Many languages were spoken across the Roman Empire and Latin was, in the main, the language of law, politics, and the military. Brevity of speech often aided communication.

He boarded the boat and greeted Regulus with great enthusiasm.

"Regulus are you well this bright spring morning?"

"I am, Gabo, the boat is ready to leave when you give the order."

"Excellent, and I have a surprise for you today. You will take charge of the voyage and take us down to Portus Piscium. You've had two years of training and experience on board, so it is time for you to step up."

Regulus wanted to throw his arms around Gabo. He had worked and waited for this day since he had first seen the boat as a child. For years he had looked to Gabo as a father figure, who had taught him so much: taking him out to hunt and fish, teaching him the rudiments of writing and arithmetic and how to read the charts and tabulations of the river and the tides.

"Thank you, I will not let you down," said Regulus.

Gabo clapped him on the shoulder.

"I know you won't, now jump on the steering oar and get us under way."

"Yes sir," said Regulus, barely able to contain himself as he took up position on the raised platform at the back of boat and began to give the commands.

"Let go the forward line, rowers in position."

The front of the boat peeled away from the loading dock, the back line straining against the current, holding the boat in position.

"Let go the back line, rowers ready."

The boat rushed forward, and the rowers dug deep in the water. The river was fast and swollen by the spring rains. The rowers showed their skill and experience, working in concert with Regulus to control speed and direction as they manoeuvred around the first few tricky bends in the river. Not for the first time did Regulus admire their skill and industry. It did not seem fair to him that these slaves had not been made Freedmen when they had more than proved their loyalty to Gabo. He knew that Gabo had applied to Prefect Sextus but had been refused on the grounds that the river economy would not support the extra money needed to pay them even a small Freedman's stipend.

The appalling truth of just how much the Empire's economy depended on slave labour was a mystery to those with limited understanding of how complex systems worked. Regulus thought about his mother, who had been in servitude as a seamstress and cook to an elderly couple in Bremetenn, and only achieved her freed status through a will upon their death. Had it not been for that, he would have been born a slave and denied the free Roman status he now enjoyed. It did not make sense to him, because most freed slaves did well for themselves and others, bringing many benefits to the Empire.

The fields of the Belisama valley rolled past as the boat made its way downstream. Wetlands had been converted to farmland by systems of ditches, which drained the boggy land. Cattle and horses grazed, farm workers ploughed and sowed crops, and further along, work parties dug more land for farming. The land was rich and fertile, and the fort veterans and villagers returned good harvests along with horse rearing. Imports via a network of roads from across the Empire supplied access to a varied diet of food for most of the year.

Occasional flashes of silver leaped from the water as a few early spring salmon battled their way upstream to end their days on the spawning beds. Kingfishers, with their electric blue plumage dived and heaved themselves away from the water, small fish dangling from their beaks. The air was full of buzzing insects from an early hatch and wily trout made rings in the water as they feasted on the limitless source of food. The sun began to climb higher, and the river began to widen as the current slowed, countered by the effects of a high spring tide pushing in the opposite direction.

The fertile fields of farmland gave way to marshland, dotted with hills of higher ground and the rowers pulled harder to maintain speed. Regulus knew they must be down far enough to catch the high-water mark to ride the outgoing ebb tide into the estuary and on to the creek at Portus Piscium. There had to be enough draft of water in the creek to allow them to dock. It was a fine balance. Even Gabo, with all his skill and years of experience had been caught out, the boat stuck on a mudbank, waiting for the next tide to float. A steady pace working with the flow got the job done.

A sharp left turn wound the river around the high ground and double-backed around the other side. The ebb tide had started to flow as the ten-mile-wide estuary came into view. Posts, pile-driven into the riverbed, marked left and right of a deep channel. A cold wind blew from the southwest, and Gabo hoisted the square sail, adjusting it to catch the wind. The boat picked up speed as rowers, tide, and wind worked together.

Small mounds of higher ground poked up from the vast watery expanse of the Belisama estuary, some topped with the Roundhouses of the Setantii people of the coastal region. The marshland area on the north side of the deep Belisama channel, the Fylde as it was called, had more Roundhouses on raised ground. The Roman Hill Fort stood high on a hill in the distance, dominating the area. Regulus steered with care as the guard on the front swung a lump of lead on a rope, checking the depth of the water and shouting measurements.

A wooden jetty came into view, jutting out of the Portus Piscium creek. A lone petite figure stood on the end of the jetty, anticipating the arrival of the boat. Regulus recognised her wild mop of long red hair and felt butterflies in his stomach, imagining her bright green eyes looking at him. It was Sabina, the woman who never failed to fascinate him and hold his undivided attention. Everything about her radiated energy and sparkle despite her low existence as a slave. He wanted to talk to her, but he was a Roman and she was a slave, a major obstacle in the stratification of Roman society. For now, though, he had to focus on getting the boat safely on the jetty while there was still enough depth of water in the creek. He steered the boat ten yards up the creek and bumped alongside the jetty.

Other slaves had arrived on the jetty, helping with the lines to secure the boat. Sabina seemed to lead the action, initiating things and one step ahead of the rest.

"Sabina, always running, always running. Doesn't she ever stop?" thought Regulus.

What he did not know was that Sabina always wanted to stay one step ahead of her slave master, the obnoxious and sadistic Stultus. It was her way of regaining a sense of control and autonomy in her otherwise owned life. It meant that he could not tell her what to do because she had already done it, and she knew that annoyed him.

One step behind as usual, came Stultus walking down the wooden walkway to the jetty from a huge warehouse on top of some higher ground. With him came the slave owner of the Portus Piscium, Festus Crassus. Together, they could be mistaken for a bizarre circus act. Festus bowled onto the jetty, a man with a girth that appeared to exceed his height, his head as bald and shiny as a steel helmet and tiny eyes sunk deep into his blubbery humourless jowls. Stultus, scrawny and gnarled with a face like a blunted battle axe and an evil grin, which showed his missing and rotten teeth. He had furtive eyes that darted around everywhere, and he carried a blood-stained multi-strap flog in his right hand, caressing the leather straps with his left.

Stultus sat down on a barrel watching the slaves work as Festus and Gabo looked over the manifest, and Regulus started to fill in the log with details of the voyage. The slaves began to carry the goods up the wooden walkway to a gravelled square in front of the warehouse. Stalls were laid out ready for bartering and selling. A crowd of Sentantii had gathered from all over the estuary and the Fylde. Boxes of fish, including the prized salmon, were stacked in front of the warehouse ready to exchange for the goods from Brematenn.

As the last of the goods were being unloaded from the boat, one of Festus's slaves stumbled and dropped a sack of bread. Stultus stood and began to flog the slave. Regulus ran over and grabbed the flog.

"Leave him alone!" shouted Regulus.

Stultus squared up, "Make me!".

Regulus shoved him hard, and Stultus reeled back before rushing at Regulus, head down, and the two of them grappled on the muddy jetty, the occasional fist flying. Just when it looked like a bit of a street scuffle, Stultus broke free and pulled his knife. Regulus responded and pulled his knife. Gabo grabbed Regulus from behind, pulled him away, and thundered at him.

"What do you think you're doing? I trust you with charge of the boat and you insult me by getting into a knife fight with an idiot!".

Regulus was shaking with anger and adrenalin. Then he noticed Sabina staring straight at him. He stared straight back over Gabo's shoulder. Gabo noticed and exploded.

"Oh, I see, not content with getting into a knife fight, now you want to be led around by your ballista bolt. Birdbrain!".

"Yes, but…".

"Shut up! Right, get on the boat and clean it from top to bottom. You'll be a real hero with the slaves then and don't even think about taking charge of the boat again until you've learned to behave like a man."

Stultus walked past and snarled at Regulus. Regulus blew him a kiss.

Gabo turned to Festus.

"My apologies, Festus, my cadet is inclined to forget himself."

"It is nothing, a mere misunderstanding. My slave master can be a little heavy-handed from time to time. Let us move on to matters of commerce," said Festus.

Regulus was left alone on the boat with a bucket of water and a scrubbing brush for company.

"Psst!"

He looked round. Sabina stood on the jetty opposite him.

"Sabina, what are you doing here. You're liable to get in trouble for talking to me."

"I don't care. I hate that sadistic idiot and I thought you showed courage standing up to him."

"I acted without thought. I won't make the same mistake again."

"You learn fast. Next time, push him in the creek."

He laughed, "Not a bad idea."

"I must go. Festus gets agitated if he can't find me," she said.

"I hope to see you again very soon," said Regulus.

"All things are possible if the gods will it. Stay well."

"And you."

She sprinted up to the market square. Regulus scrubbed away. To the west, the sun was lowering, and the tide had receded revealing a wide landscape of marsh grass with rivulets of seawater trapped in random crevices. The *Belisama Cygnus* perched on a ledge of mud at the side of the creek. The creek was revealed by the receding tide as a muddy rough shaped V, twenty feet deep with a flat bottom of silt three yards wide. Shallow fresh water from an inland brook flowed along the bottom and out into the deep channel of the Belisama. Birds filled the sky and hopped around the mud banks and marsh grass; rich pickings left by the outgoing tide.

To the east, the Pennine Hills cut a dark purple backdrop overlooking the flat marshes and river channels. The Hill Fort to the north was lighting up with torches. A full moon began to appear from behind the Pennine Hills and braziers had been lit in the market square. The sound of laughter and conversation drifted down from those who had stayed late at the market to enjoy some social drinks, although most had gone home, fearful of evil spirits and monsters said to roam the marshes and the sea at night.

Regulus washed himself from a barrel of water and walked up to the market square. Gabo was sat at a long table with Festus and two Setantii elders. Accounts and the cargo manifest littered the table along with cups, bowls, and food.

"Regulus, have you finished your work?" said Gabo.

"Done sir, may I eat?"

"Yes, come and sit down."

"Thank you, I have prepared the boat for loading at first light."

"Excellent, Festus and I have been discussing how good the trading has been today."

Festus grunted his approval and carried on eating.

The sun went down in the west, casting the last of its rays as the full moon began to spread its silvery glow over in the east. Stars littered the night sky, sparkling and blinking. The North Star shone, a distant lighthouse in the heavens accompanied by the seven sisters, who danced around it in a slow-moving plough-shaped formation. In the market square, a few stragglers warmed themselves around braziers. Festus excused himself and went to his quarters in the warehouse with the two Setantii elders. Gabo and Regulus decided it was time to turn in for the night.

To the side of the warehouse, there was a long and narrow wooden shed. Inside, on small beds with straw mattresses, the slaves slept – a cramped and filthy dormitory. There was no personal space, the slaves dispossessed of everything including their freedom. However, the standard chains and locks so prevalent at most slave camps were missing; the marshes and tides did that job. A few had tried to escape. All had failed, many caught out by the tides. Others had been caught after becoming stuck on a mudbank or turned in for reward money. One hapless slave had tried and failed three times only to end his days hanging from a cross.

Sabina had crept outside the shed as she did most nights. She enjoyed the fresh air and open space, which gave her a sense of freedom. She had been watching Regulus and Gabo and listening to their conversation. But the thing that fascinated her the most was how the moon and tides were inter-related, how the moon waxed and waned and how the tides were high or low. She had no idea why things happened that way, except that they did, and although she had received no formal education, she was quick and perceptive.

She knew she had recently changed from a girl to a woman. Soon Festus would want to realise on his investment. He told her that he had bought her six years ago at a slave market in Deva along with another girl, knowing that one of them would probably die before reaching adulthood. Plagues, fever, and crippling accidents were everyday hazards, and all but the strongest children died young. Sabina's "little sister" as she called her died from a fever six months after arriving at Portus Piscium. Now, having survived to thirteen years of age, she knew Festus would sell her as a strong virgin slave to a wealthy merchant or Brigante chief.

Festus always gave his "investments" high Roman names. Sabina was the name of the Emperor Hadrian's wife, and that suited his ridiculous delusions of grandeur, but it did seem to work and bring in a higher price. A higher price meant more money and money was the thing that mattered most to Festus. Money was everything: money for its own sake so he could look at it, count it, fondle it, and save it. Food came a distant second, although he was still greedy and selfish at the table. He accepted all invitations to dinners, but never reciprocated because that cost money.

Sabina continued to increase her knowledge of the terrain and tides in the event she needed to escape if Festus planned to sell her to some obnoxious man in a hellhole at the edge of the Empire, which would be just as bad, if not worse, as her current situation. She had a plan if she needed to act fast, although the hounds and slave catchers did present major problems. But the marsh grass would take her weight and if she could get to the higher ground in the east, the tide would cover her tracks and scent. Timing would be crucial.

On the other hand, she might be bought by a wealthy merchant, perhaps assigned to cooking and serving food to guests with the possibility of at least some form of rudimentary education. Perhaps she would be treated well like the family pet, and that had to be better than Portus Piscium and the lecherous eyes of Stultus. In any event, she was determined to keep all options, limited as they were, open. She crept back inside the shed and lay down to try and get some sleep.

It was just before dawn when Regulus was woken with a prod from Gabo. The slaves had already begun loading the boat. Stultus and Festus stood on the jetty overseeing their slaves and Gabo busied himself ticking things off the manifest as they were loaded. Stultus looked a bit sheepish, his swollen left eye half closed by a shiny purple bruise. Regulus noticed his own bottom lip had doubled in size. Gabo looked at him.

"Something wrong with your lip?"

One of the slaves stifled a laugh with a cough.

"It's not funny!" Regulus protested.

One of the guards was amused.

"You'll get over it."

Regulus busied himself securing the amphorae of fish sauce.

"The curses of the Four Furies on this stuff," he muttered to himself, still half asleep and grumpy.

Once the loading was done, everyone perched wherever they could to eat. By this time, the sun had popped up from behind the Pennine Hills in the east promising a little warmth against a biting southwest wind. Scudding clouds threatened rain making the marshes look bleak and desolate. Everyone ate in silence, cupping their hands around the bowls of hot porridge trying to get some warmth and relief. Sabina ran around serving the food and collecting empty bowls.

A tidal bore appeared and rushed up the Belisama channel. Water poured into the creek, which began to fill up with surprising speed. When the boat was afloat, Gabo took command and they pulled away from the jetty out into the Belisama channel. Regulus hoisted the square sail, and the boat sped away into the distance. Sabina stood and watched, longing to be on the *Belisama Cygnus*, a free Roman citizen with at least some control of her destiny. She caught herself missing Regulus and pushed the thought to the back of her mind as a foolish flight of fancy. She was about to run up to the warehouse to get on with her usual monotonous chores when she overheard Festus.

"That's the last voyage they'll make to Brematenn," said Festus.

Stultus laughed, "I can't wait to get Regulus under my flog."

"Patience Stultus, patience. He will be our pilot slave under your control soon enough."

Festus turned and began to walk up to the warehouse.

"Come Stultus, let us prepare for the arrival of our guests."

Sabina did not run. She stood, statue still at the end of the jetty, watching the *Belisama Cygnus* disappear as the visibility deteriorated and rain drove in sideways.

Chapter Two
Time and Tide

I

While Sabina shivered in the rain at the end of the jetty, Festus was in his personal quarters, housed in part of the warehouse. Slaves clattered about in a kitchen preparing food for a feast. A long table was set in a dining area and three chairs on each side of the table waited for the guests to arrive, with Festus's chair at the head, which was a large throne-like affair made to fit his girth. The slaves worked without speaking, but they shot each other the occasional quizzical glance; it was not like Festus to spend money and host a feast.

Out on the jetty, Sabina noticed a small boat being rowed over from one of the Roundhouses. Stultus and the two Setantii elders walked onto the jetty as the boat came into the creek. Stultus ordered Sabina to report to Festus and she ran up to the warehouse, glad to get out of the driving rain and be warmed by the fire in the dining area.

She bowed her head and addressed Festus.

"Master Festus, I've been ordered to report."

"Yes, you are to wait on my guests. Pick two female slaves to assist," he said.

"As ordered."

Outside, four burly men walked across the square. They each wore long wool cloaks with long black hair draping down over fox fur collars, and knee length black leather boots. Long swords hung from their belts and chains of office dangled from their necks, each with a medallion indicating their tribal chiefdom. Stultus and the two Setantii elders led the way, and all were engaged in quiet conversation. Sabina caught a glimpse of them as they entered the warehouse and headed to Festus's quarters. Her first thought was that she was to be paraded at the feast so a price could be agreed for her sale, and she tried to comfort herself with the thought that things could be worse.

Festus gave the men a warm welcome, pouring each a large goblet of wine with great munificence and flourish as he assured them that food was on the way. He proposed a toast.

"Men, to confederation!" and they all drank.

They took their places at the table. Stultus stood at the door, hoping beyond hope to be invited to join them for the feast.

"Close the door behind you Stultus," said Festus.

Sabina and two slave girls had washed themselves as best they could from a barrel of cold water. They tied their hair back and put on clean tunics, which Festus had ordered for them. The girls had a little giggle at each other – joy was hard to come by in the grey monotonous life of a slave. They made their way to Festus's quarters. The ever-lecherous Stultus stood outside the door leering at them as they stood waiting to be called for service. Festus opened the door and ushered the slaves inside.

They began serving the varied food, all arranged on silver platters by the kitchen slaves. Salmon, olives, venison, bread, and flounder graced the table, and the tribal chiefs ate heartily. Sabina skipped around the table, topping up the wine goblets, watching the other two girls serve food, correcting them if they made a mistake; they were nervous. The wine began to take effect and the men started to slur. One man, representing the Caledonians and the other tribes north of the Stanegate Road turned to Festus.

"If confederation of all the northern tribes turns out to be as good as this food, I can't wait," he said.

The Brigante chief chipped in, "We should have done it years ago."

One of the Setantii elders shouted out.

"We're in all the way; we should eat and drink like this every day."

The men thumped the table, cheering and roaring with laughter.

Festus stood and called the men to order for a short speech.

"Men, soon we will have control of the roads and smaller forts from the estuary of the Belisama on the west coast of Britannia to the Abus Fluvius on the east coast. By the time the legions find out, they'll be cut off. You, Brigante chief, shall have your revenge for your rebellion that was so brutally put down four years ago by Governor Falco. Emperor Hadrian will be forced to negotiate his border plans. United, you, the tribes of northern Britannia, will have a prosperous confederation, free from the corruption that is Rome. Men, to the confederation!".

They stood and shouted as one.

"The confederation!".

The room buzzed with conversation and laughter. The Brigante chief grabbed Sabina around the waist.

"Come here, perhaps I should make Festus an offer for you. Festus, is she yet a woman?"

"She is and without blemish."

"Is that what she told you?" and the other men laughed as Sabina snapped at him.

"Sir, I guard my honour with my life!"

The Brigante chief looked taken aback.

"Well now, you're a feisty little thing. Good, I like women with fire and fight and I'll see about a price for you tomorrow."

Festus was half-drunk, but he still had the presence of mind to see which way things were going.

"Slaves, you have served us well, you are dismissed. Men, let us discuss confederation matters further."

The men groaned in protest.

"Come on Festus, we want some fun with the girls," said the Caledonian chief.

Festus ordered the slaves out and ordered Stultus to take them to the slave shed.

Sabina was horrified by what she had heard. This was not one tribe rebelling against Rome, it was half of Britannia planning war on a scale not seen since Boudica. And everybody knew how that one ended. She remembered the Brigante rebellion ending in defeat four years ago when she was still trying to get used to life at Portus Piscium. The Setantii had stayed away from the fight, but she remembered the horrors: half-dead enslaved Brigantes dragged in chains, floggings, executions, crosses everywhere striking terror into the slaves, and the constant gossip of slaughter on the battle fronts.

"Insurrection and succession from Rome; what did they think they were doing?" she thought.

Worse still, she knew that if the Brigante chief bought her, she would be his slave on the losing side and, in all reasonable probability, sold as a sex slave to the salt mines or stone quarries. If Festus did not sell her, she would be the slave of a Roman traitor; an insurrectionist and she would be executed along with her master, crucified as an example.

"Could they win?" she wondered.

Then she remembered her early years as a slave in Deva and seeing the Legio XX marching and training.

"No!" she whispered to herself.

She resolved to escape that night. She filled her leather flask with fresh water, and sat on the edge of her bed, deep in thought. She knew where the moon would be over the Pennine Hills, which would be the start of her race against the spring tidal bore. Once across the marsh grass to higher ground, she would follow the Belisama to Bremetenn where she planned to surrender to the Romans and tell the Prefect what she had overheard. She also made up her mind that if she stayed a passive slave, she would live a grey pointless existence: a nonperson living in fear until the day she died, which would be sooner rather than later.

Stultus was outside, shuffling about on his rounds as night began to fall. He was the worse for wear from all the left-over wine, and rich left-over food scooped from the table. Sabina waited for things to quieten down save for the snoring of the other slaves. She sneaked out into the cold night air, just as she had done for years. There was no one around except the night guard on the jetty, marching up and down with his usual thirty pace rhythm. The moon was almost at the correct angle and Sabina pointed at its base.

"Not quite there yet," she thought.

She watched the night guard marching up and down the jetty. Thiry paces, stamp, turnabout, thirty paces, stamp, turnabout, with relentless rhythm. She had to get the timing right: the angle of the moon, the tidal bore, the marching guard, and when to run once she was over the creek. If she were too early, Stultus and the two slave drivers would catch her before the tide had cut them off; too late and she would be stuck and outrun by the tide out on the marsh. A cloud drifted over the moon as if to thwart her plans.

"Cack!" she whispered.

The cloud drifted off on its way and the moon popped out again. She pointed at its base. Now. The guard turned, stamped, and marched with his back to her as she broke the cover of the slave shed and ran down the grassy slope, avoiding the walkway and clinging to the shadows. She ducked down in the marsh grass. Thirty, stamp, turnabout, and march. Onto the jetty behind the guard, quiet as death, slithering crabwise down the muddy slope of the creek to the bottom. She flipped over onto her belly and froze. Thirty, stamp, turnabout, and march. She slipped across the quivering silt and mud at the bottom of the creek on her belly, spreading her weight, legs pushing like a frog, hands and arms pulling. It was only three yards across, but crossing seemed to take an eternity, the unstable ground threatening to swallow her with every move she made. She reached the opposite slope and heard the guard turn again.

She half ran and half clawed up the muddy slope and lay flat in the marsh grass at the top. Stamp, turnabout, and march. She crawled along the marsh grass, listening to the steady rhythm of the guard, moving only when she thought he would be unsighted. She peered round and saw she was about a hundred yards away, looked up at the moon, stood and ran. She did not sprint. She kept a steady pace, skipping over the crevices that ran between the clumps of marsh grass.

The guard, half asleep from an uneventful watch, thought he saw something move on the other side of the creek. He dismissed it as a deer, or perhaps a stray dog. Then he caught a glimpse of a human outline in the moonlight. He shouted, ran up to the warehouse square, and rang the general alarm bell. Stultus, guards, and slaves poured out of the warehouse and the slave shed. Stultus and two other slave drivers blundered about, hungover from all the wine. Stultus quizzed the guard as Festus barrelled out of the warehouse.

"What did you see?" demanded Stultus.

"It looked like one of the slaves running away towards the east – on the other side of the creek," said the guard.

"Are you sure?"

"It's dark, but I saw someone running. Do a head count, you'll soon find out."

All the slaves were marshalled into the square. Festus began the head count, glancing at all the faces. He got to number five and stopped. At that moment, he knew.

"Stultus, it's Sabina. Get the hounds and get after her."

Stultus protested, "Festus, the tide."

"Stop blathering about the tide and get after her, I want her alive, not drowned."

"But..."

"Get over the creek and bring her back!"

Two slave drivers appeared with three hounds. There was shouting and barking as Stultus, and the slave drivers jumped off the jetty and ran down the slippery side of the creek. They began to wade across the middle. Within two steps, everything came to a halt. The three men were stuck mid-thigh deep in the mud and silt. One of the hounds had refused and scampered back up to the jetty. It crouched down and barked at the scene. The other hounds were stuck up to their bellies, back legs thrashing trying to break free and making a dire situation worse. One of the slave drivers tried to lever himself out by pushing down on one of the hounds only to get bitten by the distressed animal.

Festus was screaming at them to get out and he ordered the slaves to get a rope and planks. The slaves ran around, panic stricken, as the tidal bore rushed up the Belisama channel. Water poured into the creek. Stultus panicked and tried to climb on one of the slave driver's shoulders, which pushed the slave driver in further. The slave driver punched Stultus in the face and a farcical mud-spattered fight erupted, hounds yelping, as three slaves slide down with a rope and planks. Stultus grabbed the rope and pulled one of the slaves into the water. The slave let go and crawled back. The yelping stopped. The water rose and flowed faster. The three men were trapped, up to their chests in water.

The slaves made another attempt with the rope, trying to explain and reason with the slave drivers to calm down and wrap the rope around their bodies, one at a time, but desperate self-preservation had made them deaf to reason. Stultus and the two slave drivers lurched at the rope, trying to shove and punch each other out of the way. The water rose and flowed faster. Then there was screaming, begging, thrashing at the water, until an unnerving silence fell on the scene. Three men, the abused who turned abusers, drowned, and entombed in a marsh creek. The tide rose and flowed like nothing had happened.

Sabina had heard the commotion but dared not look back as she focused on every step. The full moon pulled her along and rolled up the tide behind her. She hardly noticed the sudden silence as the tidal bore rushed up the Belisama channel on her right. She swam across a narrow creek, working sideways with the fast-flowing current until she reached the other side, then running on towards the higher ground.

Thoughts raced through her mind as she urged herself forward.

"Must run harder, faster, the hounds, the tide, Stultus...run Sabina, run for your life."

The ground began to rise and become firmer, and it was only then that she noticed there was no barking or shouting. She assumed the tide had cut them off, that they would wait until daylight and the receding ebb tide before resuming the search. Most of the past escape attempts had ended with a drowned body turning up a day or two later, but she knew they would not give up searching especially because Festus would be furious at the financial loss, driven on by the hope of finding her alive.

At last, she was on the side of a hill, the river taking shape as the tide rose. She flopped into the grass, her lungs heaving, and looked back over the estuary for the first time. She took a few gulps of water from the leather flask, gasping for breath between each gulp, and then forced herself up, running along the higher hilly ground, following the moonlit bathed Belisama.

II

Regulus looked back at Sabina as he manned the sail and she stood on the end of the jetty. A wet and windy squall blew across the boat, and the Portus Piscium began to fade from view. He wished Sabina could be with him, a free Roman woman, and wondered if he would ever have enough money to buy her freedom, knowing that Festus would demand a high price for his investment.

"Maybe one day," he said to himself.

"What?" said Gabo.

"Nothing."

"Good, now focus on the sail, the weather is closing in."

They sailed on, the rowers pulling with the wind and tide pushing them along out of the wide estuary, winding their way around the hills of higher ground. On their right side, they sailed past the "Arma Officinas", the main warehouse for official Roman armaments along with a small Roman camp and settlement. Two furnaces poured smoke and out of their chimneys, and the relentless sound of hammering that accompanied the production and repair of the machinery of warfare drifted across the river. Some children waved at them as the Belisama Cygnus sailed past, playing at skimming stones on the water, oblivious to the chilly wind and driving rain.

The river water started to turn brackish as the tidal water mixed with the fresh water flowing downstream. The current slowed and the wind from the sea began to drop as they became sheltered by the hills. Gabo gave the order to drop the sail. Regulus went to release the rope from the jam as the first volley of arrows fell from the sky. The guard on the front of the boat dropped his shield and went over the side, clutching an arrow stuck in his throat. Gabo let out a cry of pain, an arrow stuck through his right arm.

The slaves dived for cover. The second guard rushed forward and held his shield over Gabo. Gabo let go of the steering oar and the boat veered sideways in the river. The second volley of arrows rained in, but most flopped into the sodden flapping sail. One stuck in a rower's thigh. Regulus pounced on the dropped shield and rushed to the raised deck at the back. He grabbed the steering oar with one hand, holding up the shield with the other as he wrested control of the boat.

"Row now or we die!" he shouted to the rowers.

One of the rowers jumped up and took position, encouraging the rest to follow.

A third volley of arrows splashed around the boat as the range had changed. A few thumped into the woodwork. Two stuck in Regulus's shield. The rowers pulled with all their strength at a brutal tempo, and the wounded rower started to faint. The guard gave Gabo his shield and relieved the wounded rower. The boat picked up speed and the next volley of arrows fell in the water behind them. Oddly, the assailants stayed hidden in a reedbed and did not give chase. The arrows stopped as fast as they had started, and the tired rowers slowed to a steady pace.

At a straight section of the river, Regulus strapped the steering oar in position and walked over to the mast. He lowered the sail and raised the distress flag.

The sooner it was seen by the soldiers at fort, the sooner an escort could be raised for the voyage back to Bremetenn. Everyone was on edge, until the marshy ground began to give way to drained farmland. Three cavalrymen appeared on the riverbank, and they trotted along with the boat, their long swords drawn and ready. Another cavalryman appeared and immediately galloped off towards Bremetenn. Everyone on the boat was still nervous even as they rounded a corner, and they could see the flags of the fort.

Regulus turned to Gabo, "Hold on, we're almost there."

"Focus on getting us safe," said Gabo in a croaky voice.

The loading dock and the fort came into view as they rounded the last bend. Regulus could not believe his eyes. A crowd of villagers lined the top of the riverbank, soldiers in full battle kit stood in formation on the loading dock with Primus Pilus Decimus and Prefect Sextus in front of them. It seemed news travelled fast in the Belisama Valley, and bad news was no exception. The boat bumped alongside the loading dock and the rowers made the mooring ropes secure. Sextus and Decimus stepped onto the boat, and all the soldiers bolted to attention with a collective, "Hail Caesar!".

Silence followed, broken only by tweeting birds and the babbling of the Belisama. Sextus walked up and down the boat, stone-faced. He looked at the arrows that were stuck in the woodwork and spoke in an authoritarian voice.

"Pirates and bandits, they will pay for this."

"I don't think so," blurted Regulus before he realised he was out of order to a Prefect.

"You! Explain!" commanded Sextus.

Regulus bowed his head.

"Prefect Sextus, I beg your pardon, but the attack was well disciplined. The range was accurate first time, they knew when and where to attack, and they knew we were coming."

"Very good, so you're a military expert. Who do you think organised this masterpiece ambush?" said Sextus, not without a hint of sarcasm.

"I don't know sir but look at the arrows. They are Roman."

Sextus pulled an arrow out of the mast and looked at it with a critical eye.

The guard on the boat spoke up.

"Permission to speak Prefect."

"Very well, speak."

"Sir, the way they attacked us, well - it takes a long time to train archers to be so accurate and co-ordinated in the legions - they chose their cover well too."

Sextus nodded, somewhat in agreement.

"Very well, we shall investigate further, Primus Pilus Decimus."

"Yes, Prefect Sextus."

"See to it all cargo is bonded and secured in the fort, all arrows collected and brought to me. Have Fluvius Gabanator and the slave taken to the infirmary."

Sextus turned to Regulus.

"Cadet, see to it the slaves scrub the boat when the unloading is completed and make repairs."

"I will Prefect Sextus."

"You have shown courage and resourcefulness today, but next time, try to control your tongue."

"I will, my apologies Prefect Sextus."

Sextus left the boat at a brisk march. The crowd on the riverbank began to disperse, conversation buzzing as the inevitable rumours and gossip started. The loading dock and the boat burst into a hive of activity, supervised by Decimus. Seren had watched the whole scene unfold from the top of the riverbank, and she was relieved to see her son unhurt. She wished he had taken an apprenticeship with the blacksmith, or a few doors down with the baker. Still, at least he had not run off to join one of the legions or sold himself to a Lanista to train as a gladiator where prospects were, more often than not, limited.

Soldiers had been ordered to double the guard. An uneasy quiet descended over the fort and the village. The guards were on edge and extra vigilant. The Romanised Brigante in the village were worried because civilians never fared well in the event of trouble. They went about their business as twilight came to Bremetenn and the Belisama Valley.

III

Birdsong announced the impending arrival of dawn. Two guards beat a rhythmical march up and down the loading dock after a monotonous uneventful four hours of watch duty, both looking forward to food and sleep when the relief watch presented themselves. One of the guards saw something move a few feet along the riverbank at the water's edge. He recoiled and drew his sword, "show yourself!". The other guard ran over, sword in hand. A weak voice called to them, and a figure moved forward. The guards thought it was something that had crawled through the earth from the lower bowels of Hades. It was a woman, caked in mud, red hair matted across her face, and blood dripping from thorn scratches. She fell to her knees; hands raised in surrender.

"I am Sabina, slave to Festus Crassus of the Portus Piscium, I surrender to you, and I come to warn you of a plot. I beg you to take me to your Prefect."

Both guards were aghast. They seized her, dragged her up to the fort jail, and threw her in a cell. The iron door slammed, and the lock clicked. Sabina crawled to a corner, rolled up in a defensive ball, and cried deep heart wrenching sobs.

Sextus was awake early after a fitful sleep. Events from the previous day tumbled through his mind. Was this a random attack or the start of something bigger? He looked at the arrows on his desk, all of them Roman. He knew he must draft a report to Falco, the governor of Britannia. He had deployed scouts and spies across the Bremetenn district. Sextus knew he needed more information. There was a knock on the door.

"Enter."

Two guards walked in and snapped to attention.

"Yes, what is it?" said Sextus in a quiet formal voice.

One of the guards reported.

"Prefect, we have arrested an escaped slave. She says she is the property of Festus Crassus, that she surrenders to Rome, and she comes to warn us of a dangerous plot, er, also, she was ranting something about Festus Crassus and the northern tribes forming an alliance, begging us to listen."

"I see, where is she now?" asked Sextus.

"We have locked her in a cell."

Sextus sat down and put his index finger to his forehead.

"Well, now I've heard it all - an escaped slave turns herself in to warn us of a plot, unified tribes, her master in on the whole thing…" he paused, "bring her here and send for Decimus."

The guards saluted and left.

Decimus was at the door within two minutes. Sabina was behind, cuffed and chained between the two guards. She knelt on the stone floor and bowed her head in silence. Sextus stood and looked down at her.

"Slave, what have you to say?"

Sabina told him all she had overheard: Festus, the threat to the Belisama Cygnus, the feast with the chiefs of northern Britannia, and how she feared the slaughter that war would bring.

Sextus began to question her.

"What does Festus hope to gain?"

"Money, and a position of power in a confederation of tribes."

"Which roads have been set for ambush?"

"All of them north of the Belisama."

"Hmm, word will reach Deva and Legio XX."

"But they plan to take all roads and forts before word gets to them."

"Then what?"

"With the forts and roads secure, they want to force negotiation with Emperor Hadrian – I didn't catch everything, something about building a border across the north of Britannia."

The Romans looked at each other in astonishment. Sextus wondered how a slave woman from a minor fishing port could know. There had been rumours and there was to be a state visit in the summer, but no official news to date.

"When do they plan to attack the forts?" demanded Sextus.

"I don't know."

"Think!"

"They didn't talk about a date – they said something about it being imminent, and the Setantii attacking the Hill Fort and the boat."

"You are a liar; the boat is here in one piece. Tell me the truth."

"I'm not lying, I'm glad the boat made it through."

"Made it through what?"

"I don't know."

"You are lying again, how dare you come here with a cooked-up story about rebellion, insurrection, and you dishonour your master."

"I'm telling you the truth," cried Sabina.

"No, I should have you tortured, then we will get to the truth."

Sabina fell forward, hands and face flat on the stone floor, shaking with fear.

"I swear to you, I speak the truth, have mercy, please, you're all in grave danger."

Sextus paused, mindful of the unreliability of information extracted under torture. Even the most resilient would say anything to stop the excruciating pain, often begging for death. He decided on a different approach that had served him well in the past.

He instructed his guards.

"This slave is filthy. And she stinks. Take her to the bath house and order Astrid to supervise her bathing."

"Yes Prefect. Then what?"

"I shall make arrangements."

The guards saluted and marched Sabina out of the room.

"Primus Pilus Decimus."

"At your service Prefect Sextus."

"Send for Lyra."

Chapter Three
Lyra

Lyra's earliest memory was of being stood on a wooden platform under a pristine blue sky. It was baking hot, with a crowd of sweating men jeering at her, some raising their hands as an auctioneer shouted prices. Obstreperous camels growled, slaves clanked around in chains, whips cracked, and there were constant shouts of pain. At three years old, of unknown parentage, she had been brought to the wealthy Roman city of Antioch via the Silk Road from the East. Bidding competition was fierce driven by the fact that Lyra was a beautiful child, tall for her age with straight black hair, huge deep brown eyes, and a button nose.

Paedophiles in the crowd salivated and pushed their bidding budgets to the limit, some desperately trying to raise more credit. The slave trader, who had brought her here with the rest of his stock, egged the crowd on knowing he was about to turn a large profit. He was glad he had made the long and dangerous journey from the Parthian Empire across to the Roman city, which was close to the eastern Mediterranean Sea. Banditry on the road was a constant lethal threat and many did not survive the journey.

A merchant in the bidding crowd called out.

"Double that price!"

The crowd fell silent. The auctioneer whipped round to face the merchant.

"Going once – going twice – SOLD! Next lot…"

And so a terrified little girl was led off a wooden sales platform as the merchant made payment, exchanged for a tiny scroll of ownership. He took Lyra by the hand and led her away from the boiling mass of humanity and inhumanity to begin her new life of being owned by a man she had never met, and who now had control over her life and destiny.

There had been plenty of perverted men bidding for her that day, but fortune had seen to it that a wealthy merchant called Marius was now her owner. His marriage had been childless, and he and his wife had become estranged. He still loved his wife, and, with the best of intentions, he thought adopting a child would rekindle their happiness. He called her Lyra after the star constellation and the legendary harp from the gods.

One of his slave women bought two silk tunics for Lyra, had her bathed and fed, but Lyra remained frightened and withdrawn after the experience at the slave market. She had no memory of the journey along the Silk Road from the East. Marius arranged passage on a merchant ship across the Mediterranean Sea bound for Marseille via Messina. Trading had been lucrative. He had bought jewellery, spices, opium, and silk at good prices, which would make him a handsome profit in the west of the Empire. Marius had a soft heart, but he knew how to drive a hard bargain.

The voyage across the Mediterranean Sea was uneventful, apart from Lyra's propensity to seasickness, although this subsided after a couple of days at sea. She was fascinated by the sparkling blue water and the dolphins that played with tireless energy in the white surf around the front of the boat. She wanted to jump over the side and join in the fun. The slave woman entrusted to look after her was run off her feet as she began to come out of herself, laughing and playing as children do. However, things did not go so well with Marius and his wife. She wanted nothing to do with Lyra and would only agree to let her stay on the condition that she remained in service as a slave. Marius was disappointed. Lyra learned, at an age when no child should, how cruel people could be. Marius and his wife became more estranged.

Marius dotted on Lyra like she was his own daughter. He bought a learned Greek scholar slave to tutor her, and she showed uncommon academic ability: Greek, Latin, Mathematics, Philosophy, Music – Lyra applied herself and grew into a lively mischievous young woman. But it was away from the table and chair of study that she showed her real talent. She learned how to persuade and influence people, charming them within seconds of meeting and probing even the most introverted. Then there was the fact that she had grown into a statuesque stunner, attractive to men and women. Marius employed a chaperone, but even she fell under Lyra's spell.

Lyra continued to develop her skills. She watched and learned when she waited on at lavish dinner parties and official occasions, which Marius hosted at his villa. She soon learned the mores and etiquette of Roman society, watching body language and listening to what people really meant underneath what was spoken. It did not take her long to know all about who was sleeping with who and what went on behind closed doors. She also began to realise that she was equally attracted to men and women, and she indulged her appetites with male and female lovers.

By the time she reached her eighteenth birthday, she was confident in the knowledge that she had received a first-class all-round education. Bejewelled and wrapped in the surroundings of an enchanting villa overlooking the azure Mediterranean, her life of privilege and indulgent mischief seemed destined to continue until calamity came thumping on the door.

Marius was a shrewd businessman, but he was a hopeless administrator and too trusting of his accounts clerk until he discovered that the clerk had been falsifying the books and syphoning off money that should have been set aside to pay taxes. To Marius's consternation, the taxes had become long overdue, and the clerk had absconded with the money and his estranged wife. He did not have anywhere near enough ready cash to settle things. He tried and failed to use his influence with the Marseilles magistrate to play for time and arrange credit.

Roman tax authorities moved against him. All his assets were seized in the name of the emperor Hadrian to be sold at auction and that included his slaves. Marius found himself friendless and in prison. Lyra found herself under the auctioneer's hammer, stood on a wooden platform for the second time in her life.

Sextus was in Marseilles on his journey to Britannia to take up his new posting as Prefect of Bremetenn. His wife had died three months before during a plague and Sextus was in the market for an educated slave woman who would be capable of entertaining important Roman guests. Sextus was an army man and clueless when it came to the required etiquette and courtly procedures of

Roman society. He had read the pre-release information of the Lots and Lyra caught his attention. He made arrangements with the auctioneer just before the bidding started and Lyra was taken off the platform. The crowd groaned with disappointment at the obvious fix, so the auctioneer created a well-timed distraction by announcing the sale of a prize champion gladiator.

The journey through Gaul and across the raging sea to Britannia was long, cold, and wet. They trundled up the bumpy gravel roads to Bremetenn. Lyra was unimpressed. As some had noted before her, it seemed like the whole island was locked in a perpetual state of winter. She agreed. Sextus arranged a comfortable apartment for her in the village overlooking the Belisama and ordered her to arrange and furnish the dining area for dinner parties and other meetings that required the appropriate entertainment of important guests. Lyra began to make herself at home.

Of course, it did not take long for her to get back to her usual antics. Sextus was no match for her, and she soon had him seduced by her charms and under her spell. He made her a Freedwoman, but she was still tied to him in service by indentures. She proved herself away from the simple protocols of service at dinner parties, and began to show talent for conducting interrogations, something that Sextus found invaluable. The information she extrapolated from unsuspecting subjects was usually accurate unlike the unreliable shrieking confessions forced from victims of torture.

Now, four years after her unhappy arrival, a twenty-two-year-old Lyra stood at the door of Sextus's quarters, ready as usual to serve. He called her in, and she floated into the room.

"What can I do for you master," she said.

"There is an escaped slave over at the bath house. I want you to use all your skills to interrogate her. It is imperative that I know if she's telling the truth."

"Has she been tortured?"

"No."

"Ah, good. What has she told you?"

Sextus told Sabina's story. Lyra began to ask questions.

"How did she know about the boat?"

"She overheard Festus and Stultus talking just as the boat had sailed for Bremetenn."

"Hmm, do we know why she came here other than to warn us?"

"Not really, although she claims to be on the Roman side of things."

"Seems odd for a slave from such a bleak outpost."

"I know. You'd think she would want to get as far away as possible."

"Does anything make you think she might be telling the truth?"

"I'm not sure, she's certainly concerned for civilians in the event of a war, and she's gambled everything by surrendering to us. She had to know there was the possibility of being sent straight back to Festus."

"Is she a girl or a woman?"

"Difficult to know. At a guess, I'd say she's twelve maybe thirteen and she did look a sight, covered in dried mud. She's only small, you'll tower over her."

Lyra smiled, "I wonder what she'll make of Astrid."

Sextus half-laughed.

"Do I have your permission to go and conduct the interrogation?" she asked.

"Yes, yes of course and don't take too long about this one. Bring her here when you have finished."

"As you wish Prefect Sextus."

Sabina had never been in a bath house. She had heard about them and how the Roman bathing procedure was conducted, but as a slave at Portus Piscium, she had been denied the opportunity. The guards marched her out of the fort and along the riverbank. Smoke and sparks from the furnace poured out of the chimney of the stone building, which was a good reason to locate it away from the wooden barracks inside the fort. She was greeted by the largest woman she had ever seen, who wore a big smile to match her size. The guard stood outside as the woman ushered Sabina into a changing room.

"I am Astrid, the head slave attendant for women bathers. Remove your clothes to prepare for bathing," she said with a matter-of-fact Germanic accent.

Astrid took Sabina's tunic and sandals to the furnace room and threw them on the fire. She showed Sabina into the sweating room. At first, Sabina recoiled, taken aback by the steaming hot air and the heated tiled floor. Sweat poured out of her as Astrid instructed her on how to rub oil all over herself and scape the sweat and dirt off with a strigil, a blunt hooked blade. It took several goes, with intervals of soaking in a hot pool to get so much ingrained dirt out of her pores and hair. Then Astrid took Sabina to the warm room and plaited her hair like her own blond plaits in the Roman style.

Sleep began to descend on Sabina, but she was astonished by the barrel arch construction of the building that supported the high doomed ceiling. The walls were covered with frescos: various exotic and erotic images in shades of red, green, and purple. She was drawn to the painting of a nude man grinning at her and boasting a giant phallus.

Astrid noticed her staring and laughed.

"Don't worry my little bird, they're not that big in real life."

Sabina began to feel a little better, fascinated by how smooth her skin felt.

The door of the room opened, and Lyra entered. She walked over to Sabina and perched next to her on the warm tiled bench. Sabina was stunned by her naked beauty and graceful movements.

"Are you enjoying the bath house?" Lyra asked, her words stepping into Sabina's ear like musical notes from the gods.

"Very much, I've never felt so clean and warm."

"Ah, I'm so pleased. Now, I have a few questions for you."

Astrid left and went through to the cold room, plunging herself into an icy pool.

Lyra produced a small glass bottle of intoxicating sweet-smelling oil.

"Now, I'm going to finish off your bathing with a relaxing massage," she purred.

Lyra let a few drops of the oil drip on to Sabina's shoulders and then started to massage her with a slow and sensual rhythm. Sabina gasped as a wave of pleasure washed through her body. Lyra began to ask questions.

"Why have you come to Bremetenn?"

"To warn you about the attacks."

Lyra stopped the massage.

"Are you sure you haven't just come to escape Festus?"

"Yes. I don't want the slaughter that would come with war. Festus and the chiefs must be stopped."

"Then tell me, what do you hope to gain for yourself?"

"I would suffer in the event of a war, slaves always do, but I want to play a part in stopping the suffering of others. Please don't stop the massage."

Lyra applied a few more drops of oil and let her fingers slip and slide a little on Sabina's back. Sabina let out a quiet moan as the pleasure began to envelope her body and she melted. Lyra stopped and continued to question.

"I still think you're just trying to save your own skin" said Lyra in a firm voice, playing things hot and cold.

"I don't want to die if that's what you mean, please don't stop."

"Tell me about the boat."

"I didn't want any harm to come to Regulus, Gabo, or the slave rowers."

"You like Regulus, don't you?

"Yes, very much."

"When do the Setantii plan to attack the Hill Fort?"

"The word they used was 'imminent'."

Lyra massaged a little more.

"You seem to be on Rome's side. Tell me why."

"Because I've always wanted to be a Romanised Briton, I want to learn, to be educated, to do some good in this world. I don't want the monotonous drudgery that stalked my childhood, the meaningless tasks, or my value being calculated according to my virgin status."

Lyra's hands began to work all over Sabina's back. Sabina put her head on Lyra's shoulder cocooned in an erotic haze and under Lyra's spell. Lyra continued to probe and question, withdrawing pleasure to solicit answers. She pressed for details of Sabina's escape, how she followed the Belisama to Bremetenn, and how she had worked out the relationship between the moon and tides. Then Lyra took Sabina to heights of ecstatic pleasure, satisfied that she had the truth from the interrogation session.

Astrid had left a new tunic and a pair of sandals for Sabina in the changing room. Lyra applied some rouge to Sabina's lips and held a mirror up for her. Sabina did not recognise herself: neat, plaited silky red hair, gleaming white skin and her lips standing out with the rouge. She almost cried at what she thought was a rebirth after her grime ridden existence out in the Belisama estuary at Portus Piscium under Festus and the sadistic cruelty of Stultus. She felt warm inside, and thanks to the skilled attentions of Lyra, she felt a contentment she had never felt before.

Lyra and the guards escorted Sabina back to Sextus's quarters. Sextus stood at his desk with his centurions pouring over a map of the roads and forts in the northwestern area of Britannia. When Lyra, Sabina, and the guard entered, Sextus ordered the centurions and the guard to leave them alone and wait for further orders. Sabina bowed her head, afraid of what might come next.

"Lyra, report and give me your assessment," said Sextus.

"In short, she's telling the truth."

Sextus sat down and tapped his index finger on the table.

"I see, are you certain?"

"Yes, and I see little point in sending her back to Festus. He will have her tortured to find out what she has told us."

"He will. Slave, I am holding you as a prisoner of Bremetennacum under the charge of Lyra…you must do as she commands as if you are her slave. Make no mistake if you try to escape you will be executed."

"Yes, Prefect Sextus."

"Dismissed!"

Lyra and Sabina left, and the centurions filed back in the room.

Lyra led Sabina to her apartment in the village. Sabina was open-mouthed at the comfortable chairs and couch recliners. Frescos lined the walls depicting Romans in reclined positions dining on a wealth of food and wine. Rich red drapes hung either side of the window with a spectacular view of the river and the south side of the valley. Late afternoon sun angled through the window giving the room a rich orange glow. She noticed a white fluffy ball on one of the chairs, which came to life apparently disturbed by Lyra clattering about in the kitchen. She had seen plenty of cats before, but they were thin mangy things that ran around catching rats. This cat was fat and hairy, pure white with a peculiar pushed in face. It sat up on the chair and looked at her looking at it. Lyra came out of the kitchen with some food and water.

"Ah, I see you've met Dido," said Lyra.

"Yes, I've never seen a cat like that before – she looks a bit peevish."

"Not at all. She's from the east of the Empire, imported from what used to be Persia."

"I see."

"Yes, many in Roman society have them as pets."

"Hmm."

"I'm sure you'll get to know each other. She can be quite affectionate when the mood takes her. Here, have some food and drink."

Sabina did not have to be asked twice. She had been running on adrenaline and fear since her nocturnal adventures the night before and she consumed the bread and flounder with relish. When she had eaten, she sat back in the chair and fell into a deep dreamless sleep. Dido decided to stroll over and curl up in her lap. Lyra sat back in her chair, collected her thoughts, and began to think.

Regulus's day had been busy attending to the boat with the slaves. It was late afternoon when he and took the opportunity to visit Gabo at the Infirmary. Seren was sat at Gabo's side dabbing his forehead with a wet cloth and giving him sips of water. The surgery performed on the wound had been brutal; the arrow quiver cut off and the shaft pulled through from the other side where the barbed head protruded. Gabo laid on the bed, cushioned by a large dose of opium. Regulus embraced his mother.

"How is he?" asked Regulus.

"He's starting to run a fever. The surgeon has given him opium for the pain and said recovery was a matter of time," said Seren.

Regulus looked at Gabo, upset to the point of tears. The slave who had also been hit on the boat limped over to pay his respects. Gabo opened his eyes and looked at the three of them stood by his bedside. He reached up and grabbed Regulus's hand.

"Regulus, listen to me. I've seen hundreds of wounds like this when I served in the Dacian campaign on the Danube, and they don't end well. If I die, there is a will filed with Prefect Sextus. You are to be Fluvius Gabanator, the slaves are to be made Freedmen, and there is some money to pay for things..." his voice tailed off into a croaky cough.

"Gabo, I must ask you – are you my real father?"

"No. Your mother and I have been close friends for years, but we are not, and never have been, lovers."

"I understand, but come on, you're as tough as a legionary's hob-nailed boot. You'll pull through."

"That may be, but I don't feel quite so tough," he said as he sank back into an opium induced doze.

Seren and Regulus sat talking in low voices as Decimus entered the Infirmary and walked over to Gabo.

"Gabo, it's me, Decimus."

Gabo opened his eyes.

"Decimus my old friend – look, a little scratch and they put me in the Infirmary. Rome's gone soft!"

"I know, it will not do. Come on, let's get the men together for a night march."

The two of them laughed.

"Take it easy my old friend. I came to wish you well."

"Thank you Decimus, you're a good man."

Regulus was struck by the human side of Decimus in an informal role. He had not realised that Decimus and Gabo were so close.

Decimus turned to Regulus.

"You are to come with me and report to Prefect Sextus."

"What's it about?"

"Prefect Sextus will explain. Follow me."

Regulus kissed his mother and followed Decimus to Sextus's quarters. He was dumbstruck to find Sabina stood in the room, especially after her makeover at the bath house. She had been woken at Lyra's apartment by a guard and escorted to Sextus's quarters. The three of them stood in silence as Sextus began to give orders:

"Primus Pilus Decimus, you are to go to the Hill Fort and inform them of Festus's plans. You will go tonight under cover of darkness."

"As ordered Prefect Sextus."

"Cadet, you will see to safe passage in a small boat down to the estuary marshes. Slave, you will go with them and guide Centurion Decimus over the marshes to the Hill Fort. Decimus will remain at the fort, you and Cadet Regulus will return to Bremetenn," said Sextus.

Sabina's eyes doubled in size. Regulus felt sick.

"Decimus, Centurion Marcellus will take your post in your absence. I'm afraid things are moving fast. Not one of the messenger riders has been through today and none of the scouts have returned to report," said Sextus.

"Prefect Sextus, permission to speak freely," asked Decimus.

"Continue."

"I have experience of operating behind enemy lines during my time with the Legio XX. It takes training and battled-hardened legionaries. A cadet and a slave all seems a bit, well, desperate."

"Desperate times, desperate measures."

Decimus stiffened to attention.

"As ordered!"

Sextus went on.

"The three of you will go in a small boat disguised as fishermen. Cadet, see to the timing of the tide and leave as soon as possible. Any questions?"

Silence.

"Dismissed!"

They went to one of the barracks and changed. Sabina wiped the rouge from her lips and unplaited her hair. Some of the soldiers looked quizzically at the three of them, but no one spoke. They went down to the loading dock dressed in long cloaks with hoods and they covered their faces with dirt, trying their best to look like Setantii fishermen. They planned to hide in plain sight, reasoning that nobody would suspect three figures fishing from a rowing boat out on the river.

Sabina broke the silence.

"Here I am again, covered in cack and preparing to go fishing out on the marshes."

"I didn't recognise you before, you looked so beautiful," said Regulus.

"Oh, so you didn't think I looked beautiful before?"

"Of course I did, it's just that er, well... how in the name of all the gods did you get to Bremetenn?"

"I'll tell you later if we're still alive."

Decimus growled at them.

"When you two lovebirds have finished billing and cooing, we need to get going."

Regulus sat at the tiller, Sabina at the front, and Decimus on the oars in the middle. They slipped away, hoods over their heads as they headed downstream driven along by the fast-flowing current of the Belisama.

They made their way in silence apart from Regulus prompting Decimus at awkward bends. They met the tidal reaches just before high water, but a wind against tide made for a rough passage.

Clouds began to obscure the moonlight and Regulus steered them along, hugging the north bank looking for a small creek, which joined an inland brook. He recognised a gap in the marsh grass that was beginning to wave just above the water as the tide receded, which revealed the entrance to the creek. Decimus pulled hard against the outflow, and they made their way up the creek. Marsh grass was now revealed, and Sabina stepped out with a rope to help pull the boat along, wading knee deep in the water. The creek became narrow, and the boat bumped on the muddy bottom in shallow water, and they all pulled the boat out of the water. It was bleak and deserted in the darkness of night, but they could see the Roundhouse fires, and the torches and braziers burning up on the ramparts of the Hill Fort in the distance.

Decimus was eager to get started.

"Slave, we must go now."

"I will lead you Primus Pilus," she said.

Sabina began to run and skip like she'd done for years on fishing trips out in the estuary marshes. Decimus galumphed after her, trying to keep pace. She led the way, finding higher dry ground wherever she could to help Decimus. The going became easier as they drew close to the Hill Fort. Decimus was still blundering along when he put his foot down a muddy crevice with a loud squelch followed by a curse.

Sabina hissed at him.

"Watch where you're going you big oaf!"

"Shut up slave! What a place this is, the gods have abandoned it."

Sabina could not help a giggle. They plunged on into the night. They were close to the Hill Fort now. Roundhouses surrounded the base of the hill. It was quiet. The Setantii did not go out much at night, spooked by stories of evil spirits and monsters in the marshes. Decimus and Sabina crouched down in the grass. Decimus waited his chance and turned to Sabina.

"Slave, wait here. When I get in the fort I will signal you with one wave of a torch, understand?"

"Yes, I understand."

"Good. Remember, you cannot be taken alive if you're caught because they will torture you until you regard death as your best friend. Put your dagger here over your heart and fall on it."

"I will remember."

"This had better work," Decimus grumbled to himself.

Sabina watched him start to walk up the hill between the Roundhouses, staying in the shadows. He was almost at the top when two Setantii men appeared from a doorway. Decimus pretended to be drunk and embraced the two men.

"Good men, come, come, have a drink with me," he implored them with enthusiasm, "I go to tell those Roman pigs what I think of them."

The two men scuttled off back in the Roundhouse, less than enthusiastic about picking a fight with Roman guards up at the fort. Decimus lumbered his way on to the gravelled area around the fort at the top of the hill and approached the front gate. Sabina watched in disbelief.

He challenged the two guards.

"Roman pigs, come and challenge me."

The guards drew swords.

"Run away or die!" spat one of the guards.

Decimus moved his hood back.

"I am Centurion Decimus of the Valaria Victrix, Legio XX. I come with news from Prefect Sextus of Bremetennacum. Arrest me now, rough me up and make it look good. Do it now."

One of the guards recognised him from Bremetenn and moved fast.

"Right Setantii pig, you're off to a cell," as he punched him in the stomach and both guards marched Decimus into the Hill Fort.

Sabina waited until she saw a wave of a torch as arranged and crawled away until she was out of the light cast from the Hill Fort. Then she ran and skipped across the marsh grass back to the creek only to find Regulus snoozing behind the boat.

"Regulus, what are you doing, wake up!"

"I'm sorry, it's been a long day," he said.

"You should have tried my day!"

They sat down to wait for the incoming tide, shivering in the cold and clinging to each other for warmth, talking about the events of a long day and two nights. Regulus listened to Sabina's escape story, admiring her courage and resourcefulness. He loved feeling her next to him and listening to her talk. They talked on as the first light of dawn began to show behind the Pennine Hills and the tidal bore rushed down the Belisama channel. They shoved and dragged the boat down a muddy bank to the water's edge. The tide rose and floated them off, and Regulus rowed them out of the creek to head back to Bremetenn, the tidal current speeding them on their way.

They were both soaking wet and cold, but inside they felt something else. They had started to get to know each other and felt some sense of achievement in that they might have played a part in stopping a devastating and bloody war. Perhaps if the Hill Fort and Bremetenn stood firm, the tribes would back off and Festus would be isolated.

But as the sun began to rise on a new day, the Fates had other ideas.

Chapter Four
Treason and Plot

Festus was oblivious to Sabina and Regulus setting off with the tide from a point two miles east of Portus Piscium. He was still furious about Sabina's escape and Stultus's idiotic failed attempt to hunt her down, and he assumed that the tide would eventually wash her up somewhere out on the marshes like most of the other escape attempts. He did not care for her welfare, counting her life only in monetary value and he offset that thought with the hope that she might have survived and be turned in by the Setantii for a reward. For now, though, he continued to study the map of the northwest area of Britannia, which was spread over the large dining area table, confident in the knowledge that all the roads had been secured.

All messengers had been killed on route between forts, ambushes set on the roads in all directions, and the horse staging posts were secure and under his control. He looked closely at the intersection of the road from the Hill Fort to Bremetennacum and its connecting road east through and over the Pennine Hills to Eboracum, South to Deva via the low tide ford at Arma Officinas, north to Calunium, and on up to Luguvallium where he suspected Emperor Hadrian would draw his border for Britannia, tracing the

Stanegate Road. His co-conspirators at the Arma Officinas further down the Belisama estuary would supply more weapons and make repairs on equipment damaged in action.

He looked away from the map to rest his eyes for a moment and reflected on his own army experience; how he had joined Legio IV Flavia Felix on his fourteenth birthday to begin training and had distinguished himself during the second Dacian war under Emperor Trajan before his twentieth birthday, commended for bravery and fighting skill, and awarded the rank of centurion. He remembered how he had been assigned to Deva to train the legionaries in tight battlefield tactics, an aspect of combat where he showed real talent. A promotion to Prefect seemed, at least in his mind, inevitable.

When promotion did come, he was sent to Portus Piscium. Here, in a desolate river estuary, he oversaw slaves in a minor fishing and shipping port. Other comrades in arms, who had not shown half his talent, had been promoted to more exciting and lucrative posts, some of whom had not yet seen active duty on a battlefield. His resentment for the way Rome had repaid him for his dedication and talent began to fester into laziness and avarice with an obsession for making and accumulating money. In Festus's mind, those that had money, got on; those that did not, did not. Resolute in that knowledge, he had turned his back on Rome to collude with the tribes of northern Britannia and build a confederation of tribal states outside the Empire.

Turning back to the map, he looked at Deva, home to the Legio XX to the south and over to Eburacum, home to the Legio VI in the east. They had to kept apart at all costs. If they united, the tribes would be faced with an army more than ten thousand strong taking the field and that, he knew from experience, spelled victory for Rome. However, kept apart with roads and forts against them, they would be harried and fragmented, pulled from one obstacle and ambush to another. Emperor Hadrian wanted defined borders to develop a Roman world of peace and culture within those borders. Festus calculated that Hadrian would negotiate and give the tribes what they wanted, or Rome would be trapped and roiled by a forever war in northern Britannia.

A slave served him his breakfast and he turned his thoughts to plans for the day. He would oversee the formation of the Setantii attack on the Hill Fort before heading over to the Trough Valley between the Pennine Hills and join the main Brigante force for the attack on Bremetenn. The other tribal leaders were now on their way to join their armies for other attacks over the next two days. For now, he allowed himself a quiet moment to content himself with the thought that all his hard work and planning was coming together.

Then the door was flung open and a Brigante cavalryman burst into the room.

"Festus, the Setantii bowmen didn't capture the Belisama Cygnus."

"What, why have they not let me know?" shouted Festus.

"I don't know, I've only just had the message relayed from one of our lookouts in Bremetenn. I came as fast as my horse could gallop," said the Brigante.

"Where is the boat now?"

"Bremetenn as far as I know."

Festus regained his composure and began to gather his maps and scrolls from the table:

"No matter, we'll take it when we take Bremetenn. Let us turn our attention to the east and see to it that the Setantii attack starts at the agreed time."

Festus went out to the gravelled market square where his horse waited, attended by two slaves. He mounted the horse and moved off slowly over uneven ground, accompanied by ten Roman guards and five Brigante cavalrymen. It was time to execute the plans.

Regulus and Sabina continued their journey out of the estuary and along the Belisama towards Bremetenn. Their disguise as two Setantii fishermen in a small boat was serving them well, even waving at Setantii as they went by. They made good time until they reached the point in the river where the downstream flow countered the incoming tide and while Regulus rowed harder to keep pace, he made little progress. He pulled the boat over to the riverbank and tied it to a tree next to a reedbed where he and Sabina hid until they were sure there was no Setantii or Brigantes in the area. It was now a matter of walking the remaining seven miles up to Bremetenn.

Regulus was especially nervous after the ambush the day before, alert for any signs of Brigante and Setantii warriors. It was slow going on the wet ground, the river often flooding the surrounding valley as this land had not yet been drained. They hid behind bushes and checked for Brigantes, not moving until they were sure their way was clear. It was almost noon before they reached drained farmland, and both began to wonder why there were no farmers or working parties in the fields.

"Everywhere is deserted," said Sabina.

"I know, looks like everyone's staying in Bremetenn," Regulus paused, "at least we've not seen any Brigantes."

"We might just get out of this alive," murmured Sabina.

"Let's not get carried away."

Despite their precarious position, Sabina liked being with Regulus. She could not help but think how ironic it was that they had finally got to know each other on a life and death mission for the Romans. She had always known that Regulus liked her and she him, but the citizen slave bar had, as it did with so many potential romances, always stood in the way. She gazed with wonder at the beauty of the clear babbling water of the Belisama and how different it was to the silty brown tidal waters of the estuary. Perhaps things were this beautiful in the afterlife. But she was also thinking about seeing Lyra, remembering the feeling of her caresses that made her ache inside and long to see her again.

Then she saw the flags of the fort.

"Regulus, look, the fort!"

They crouched down, trying to see if the Romans still had control of the fort and the village.

Regulus turned to Sabina, "I think we're going make it."

"Shush, what's that?" Sabina whispered.

"What's what?"

"Gotcha!"

They both managed a hushed laugh, like children out on a mischievous adventure.

Regulus leaned across and gave her a kiss on the cheek."

"What, you wait until we're here to do that?" she said with a blush.

"I've wanted to do that since the first day I set eyes on you."

"I wish you had and taken me away from that stinking hellhole."

"I didn't have the kind of money Festus would have demanded."

"I know – we slaves are commodities to be used, bought and sold like tools on market day."

They made their way along the riverbank to the outer ditch of the fort. On the road, they could see the villagers going about their day as normal. They walked towards the west gate until a guard spotted them and approached.

"Is that you Regulus?" said the guard.

"Yes, please take us to see Prefect Sextus."

The guard led them to Sextus's quarters. As they went, Sabina was careful to walk behind Regulus, mindful of her station. Even though she had made a success out of a critical and dangerous mission for the Romans, she was still a slave and subordinate to a citizen. The injustice of it made her angry, but she remained determined to keep her cool despite her feisty nature. Given time, she had every intention of winning her freedom and her determination to achieve that freedom supressed her frustration in the moment. For now, she was content to watch, listen, and learn, a strategy that had served her well leading up to her daring and successful escape.

Sextus's voice responded to the guard's knock on the door.

"Come!" He looked surprised to see Regulus and Sabina.

"Prefect Sextus, Primus Pilus Decimus made it into the Hill Fort," said Regulus.

"Good! Slave, what did you see?"

"Prefect Sextus, I saw one wave of a torch from the parapet, just as Primus Pilus Decimus had told me he would do when he got inside the Hill Fort," said Sabina, bowing her head.

"Excellent, although we have received bad news from one of our scouts. There is a Brigante army in the Trough Valley of the Pennine Hills. Also, I'm sorry to say Gabo is not doing well."

"Permission to see him Prefect Sextus," said Regulus.

"Yes, go, and slave, return to the custody of Lyra."

Regulus left in a hurry and ran over to the Infirmary. Seren was still sat at Gabo's bedside. Gabo looked terrible: grey sweaty skin, eyes closed, and a putrid smell hung in the air from the black infection that had spread with merciless speed from the arrow wound. He was a pale shadow of the robust, confident man who had piloted the *Belisama Cygnus* on the Belisama and seen so many battles on the Rhine and the Danube. Regulus felt like he had been punched in the stomach when he saw the man that he had regarded as a father figure and role model.

Sabina crept into the Infirmary and approached with caution.

"I thought you were with Lyra," said Regulus.

"She granted me leave to visit Gabo," she whispered.

Seren turned to them both.

"The surgeon does not think Gabo will survive the day."

Regulus's face turned to stone.

"Festus will pay for this," he said in a menacing tone.

"Anger and revenge will eat you up, don't go there," said Seren.

"I won't let that happen, but I will even the score for Gabo," said Regulus through clenched teeth.

"Take care, Regulus. Festus is a nasty piece of work and a better fighter than you might think," cautioned Sabina.

As if to punctuate the conversation and bring it to a close, Gabo breathed his last. Funeral arrangements were made in accordance with Gabo's wishes, his body placed on a pyre one boat length from the Belisama Cygnus. The pyre was lit, and smoke billowed up to the heavens as soldiers and villagers stood in silence. The rowers stood with heads bowed, saddened by the passing of a man who they had come to respect and had always treated them honourably, despite their slave status. A Roman priest from the Temple of Minerva led prayers and invocations to the gods for safe passage to the afterlife and the Elysian Fields. Seren grieved for a friend who she had loved like a brother and a guard of honour drew their swords in a salute for a fallen veteran, brother, and Fluvius Gabanator in times of war and peace. The fire raged around the pyre and burned inside Regulus.

Soldiers and villagers began to disperse as the fire calmed down. Sabina followed Lyra back to Lyra's apartment and Regulus walked home arm in arm with Seren. The rowers and some of the soldiers went to the *Belisama Cygnus* to begin preparations for an assault on Arma Officinas. Sextus and Marcellus went to the fort to finalise plans for aggressive action to take the fight to Festus and the tribes. In Sextus's quarters, they went over the plans one methodical step at a time.

The first thing to be done was to send a detachment of twenty crack veterans led by Marcellus on the *Belisama Cygnus* to take control of Arma Officinas. Second was to send marathon runners down to Mamucium and Deva; those who knew their way across the wild moorland and could avoid the road ambushes. Third was to prepare Bremetenn for defence and counterattack. They were sure an attack would come from the north since crossing the narrow bridge over the Belisama from the south would present a death trap. Fourth, they planned to house and protect the villagers in the fort barracks at the first sign of an approach by the enemy.

Preparations had begun in earnest on the *Belisama Cygnus*. Four formidable ballista machines capable of launching deadly iron balls and crossbow style bolts were nailed to the deck front and rear. Shields hung from brackets on both sides of the boat providing cover for the soldiers and rowers. Javelins, bows, arrows, and spare swords replaced the usual amphorae of oil. Regulus was about to take command of a boat that looked more like a war galley on the Danube or the Rhine. Work continued by torchlight into the early evening.

Marcellus arrived on the loading dock to inspect the work and begin issuing battle orders when one of the rowers approached him with his head bowed low.

"Centurion, may I speak with you?" said the rower.

"Yes slave, and make it quick," sighed Marcellus with impatience.

"With all respect, I have experience of fighting. I was a Dacian warrior and I fought against Rome in the second Dacian War. Let me now fight for Rome and the sacred memory of Gabo."

Marcellus laughed at him.

"Well, you can't have been that good. You lost and now you're a slave!"

All the soldiers guffawed, adding to the humiliation.

"Centurion, master, let me show you," said the slave in a quiet measured voice.

An ugly silence fell over the boat and the loading dock. The Romans regarded this as a slave challenging a Roman, something that needed to be resolved with a flogging. Two of the soldiers seized the slave, but Marcellus had another idea. He wanted to thoroughly humiliate the slave in front of everyone and demonstrate that he was still the best swordsman in Bremetenn. He grabbed a spare sword and threw it on the ground in front of the slave. There were gasps of surprise and everybody stood back. Marcellus drew his own sword and pointed it at the slave.

"Show me, slave."

The slave picked the sword up and faced off against Marcellus, bowed, and crouched down in a defensive position. With lightning speed, Marcellus went for the slave, but the slave parried the blows and countered, driving Marcellus to the edge of the loading dock, steel clashing on steel. Backwards and forwards they went, both men giving and defending with all their energy and skill with nothing to call between them. All the men on the boat and the loading dock shouted and cheered, egging the two fighters on, and laying bets as money changed hands as fast as the swords clashed. Soldiers and villagers who heard the furore lined the top of the riverbank, which provided a grandstand view of the torchlit fight.

Then Marcellus disarmed the slave with a deft stroke and twist of his sword. The slave leaped forward, grabbed, and twisted Marcellus's wrist until his sword clattered to the ground. What started as a sword challenge descended into a bruising bare-knuckle brawl, bone on bone, again with nothing to call between the two men. This raised the crowd's bloodlust, more money changing hands as the white-hot betting ramped up, the crowd carried away by a spectacle worthy of the arenas at Londinium and Deva.

Then a voice roared out above the shouting.

"Stop now centurion, or I'll have you flogged raw! Slave, stop now or I'll have you executed!"

Both men froze. Sextus stepped onto the dock. All the soldiers stood bolt to attention and the slaves dropped to their knees, heads bowed low.

"In the name of Mars, what's all this cack?" barked Sextus.

"Well, Prefect, sir, you see... "said Marcellus.

"Silence! I need good fighters, not dead ones!" ranted Sextus as he turned to the slave.

"Well slave, do you want to fight and die for Rome?"

"Prefect Sextus, I pledged my loyalty to Gabo years ago. I will gladly fight and die for Rome and in honour of Gabo's memory," said the slave, and bowed as a mark of respect.

Sextus stepped back, looked at the two bloodied men, and paused for thought. The facts were that Marcellus was the best swordsman under his command and this noble slave was every bit his equal in skill, courage, and stamina. He needed first rate fighters for the small detachment he was sending to Arma Officinas, knowing they would be outnumbered at least four to one if things came to a fight. He reasoned with himself that it would serve no purpose to flog the centurion and execute the slave. Better to let it slide as a warrior-on-warrior fight and please the assembled crowd.

He addressed the crowd with a broad gesture.

"Soldiers, slaves, citizens, these men have shown the courage of great warriors. Tomorrow, we will take Arma Officinas. Let us send Festus Crassus, that treacherous slime, and his barbarian scum to the lower bowels of Hades! We will defend Bremetenn to the last man. Hail Caesar!"

The crowd roared, "Hail Caesar!" over and over again.

He turned to Marcellus and the slave.

"Clean yourselves up. Marcellus, arm this slave when you get to Arma Officinas."

"Yes Prefect."

Regulus woke with a start, images of death and burning funeral pyres tumbling through his mind as consciousness took over from the weird world of nightmares. It was still dark and a long way from the first light of dawn, but he comforted himself in the fact that he had managed to get some sleep to meet the challenges ahead. He sat up on the edge of the bed, still in his usual stunned stupor when he heard his mother talking to someone at the door just before she came in to wake him.

"Regulus, it's Centurion Marcellus," she said.

He staggered to the front door.

"Yes centurion what is it – and what happened to your face?"

"Don't ask! You are to come with me and report to Prefect Sextus."

"I'm coming, give me a moment," said Regulus as he began gathering his things.

They walked down the road, torches burning and lighting their way. Regulus shivered, part from the cold of the pre-dawn chill and part from the weight of responsibility from the expectations of manhood. No more Gabo to advise and help. He second guessed that he was to be awarded the rank of Fluvius Gabanator according to Gabo's will, and he would be expected to take command of the *Belisama Cygnus*. He had never seen a battle let alone participate in one. True, he had been in the occasional street fight with some of the boys, but nothing on the scale he was sure he was about to face. He walked with Marcellus into the fort and on to Sextus's quarters.

Sextus stood behind his desk looking grim and haggard through lack of sleep. Oil lamps burned on the walls and lit the room with extra lamps placed around the desk, which illuminated the map of northwest Britannia and some sealed scrolls. Marcellus and Regulus stood to attention as Sextus spoke in a dry and commanding voice.

"Regulus, you are to be Fluvius Gabanator. Here is your scroll of office. Do you accept this honour?"

"Yes, Prefect, unto death," said Regulus.

"Very well, also, here is Gabo's will. In accordance with his wishes, all slave rowers are now Freedmen," said Sextus, and continued as he shuffled some more scrolls around the table, "a sealed chest has been delivered to your mother and you must give these scrolls of Freedman's status to each of your rowers."

Sextus paused and looked Regulus in the eye.

"These are troubled times. I expect you to serve and discharge your duties with courage and honour. Do not fail Rome."

"I will serve with courage and honour," said Regulus, surprised by the resolve in his own voice.

"Good. Now, you will now take the *Belisama Cygnus* down to Arma Officinas. Centurion Marcellus is in command of a detachment to secure the armoury by force if necessary."

Marcellus and Regulus bolted to attention.

"Dismissed."

Regulus and Marcellus walked in silence out of the fort and along the riverbank to join the detachment. Both knew that today could be their last and they faced it with grim stoicism as all Romans were taught to do from childhood. Torchlight still danced on the waters of the Belisama, illuminating the loading dock and the boat. Rowers were in position and the twenty soldiers waited on the boat dressed in full armour of steel helmets and chain mail. Regulus went to the locker at the back of the boat and looked at the tide tabulations corresponding to the phases of the moon. He calculated that they should get under way before first light to allow enough time to compensate for the extra weight of weapons and men in the boat. Then he took a deep breath and addressed the men from the raised platform at the back of the boat:

"I am Regulus, your Pilot. Rowers, by the will of Gabo and manumission, you are now Freedmen pledged to me by Articles of Service and honour. Centurion and soldiers of Rome, you will obey my orders while you are aboard this boat. Are we clear?"

There was a collective shout.

"Yes!"

"Very well, let go the mooring lines."

The boat sprang forward as the first flecks of dawn flickered in the east. Thoughts flashed through Regulus's mind as he imagined Gabo next to him, talking him through the first tight bends in the river. Stranger than fiction it was that his first lone command of the *Belisama Cygnus* would coincide with war between Rome and the northern tribes of Britannia. He smiled with grim gaiety at the thought that this could be his first and last command and he would be in the afterlife with Gabo.

On the riverbank, Seren stood in the shadows watching her son sail away. Next to her stood Astrid watching Marcellus, both praying for safe returns. Sabina and Lyra joined them, Sabina wondering if she was seeing Regulus alive for the last time. Lyra put a comforting arm around Sabina's shoulders, the pleasure of which clouded her emotions and made her wish she were not so attracted to Lyra. But the simple fact was that she ached for Lyra ever since the interrogation and the pull was as inescapable as gravity. Lyra, calculating as ever, turned to Sabina.

"Sabina, I've been thinking. What is Festus's greatest weakness?"

Sabina did not hesitate.

"Money."

"You're sure?"

"No doubt."

"Ah, then I have an idea," said Lyra and a crafty smile spread over her face.

Chapter Five

Arma Officinas

A tense silence fell over the *Belisama Cygnus* as it lumbered its way down the river towards Arma Officinas, loaded with soldiers and weapons, Regulus struggling to control speed and direction, and the rowers pulling hard on the oars. Marcellus stood at the front and he and all the other soldiers were alert to any movement on the riverbank and in the reedbeds that could indicate an ambush by Setantii or Brigante warriors. The ballista machines were manned and loaded, and other soldiers stood with their bows and arrows ready for action.

As they arrived at the tidal reach of the river, Setantii appeared on the riverbank, pointing at the boat, and arguing with each other, but they did not attack. Marcellus guessed the main force was pre-occupied with attacking the Hill Fort and that so a few warriors knew better than try to attack a well-armed and defended war galley. Progress was slow but steady as the river widened and the outgoing tide began to push them along, compensating for the extra weight. The billowing smoke of the furnaces at Arma Officinas soon came into view on the left side of the river. They moved towards the outline of the jetty in the distance that jutted out into the river, and they prepared to land and attack if they met with resistance.

Marcellus turned to the Dacian rower.

"Give me your name Freedman."

"Dadas, centurion."

"Are any of your rower comrades capable of fighting?"

"Yes, all of them."

"Good enough. Do you know how to skirmish around a formation?"

"Yes, I did it many times against Romans in Dacia."

"So, I will form up the soldiers to punch through the middle of the ranks while you and the other rowers skirt round the enemy flanks."

"As you order centurion. We will win your respect today."

"Arm yourselves as soon as we are secure on the jetty and wait for my command. And you'd better get this right, or we all die."

The *Belisama Cygnus* made its final approach and a cohort of eighty soldiers led by a centurion had gathered in formation at the jetty, ready to formally receive the surprise visit. Marcellus and his soldiers eyed them warily, although Marcellus was surprised by how young most of the potential opposition looked; raw recruits sent to a relatively easy post to start their service and army careers. The boat bumped alongside the jetty and Marcellus stepped ashore to address the Arma Officinas centurion and exchange formal greetings. Regulus felt his heart pounding as the two centurions went through the formalities. Then Marcellus began to explain the reason for the visit.

"Centurion, I have a sealed scroll with orders from Prefect Sextus," said Marcellus as he handed the scroll to the centurion, who broke the seal and read the contents.

"So I am to relinquish control to you at the behest of Prefect Sextus?"

"With immediate effect."

"I obey Prefect Festus Crassus so until I receive orders from him, you have no jurisdiction here."

Marcellus gave the order for his men to come ashore and form up in a line behind him. Then he addressed the centurion.

"I have my orders to take control of Arma Officinas, by force if necessary."

Swords were drawn and shields went up on both sides. The rowers jumped onto the jetty armed with swords. Regulus drew his sword and stood firm, ready to defend the boat to the death.

The Arma Officinas centurion bellowed an order.

"Attack!"

Marcellus and his soldiers formed a tight shoulder to shoulder pack and went straight for the centre of the larger opposing force. They pushed forward with their shields and stabbed over the top. The effect was devasting on the young and inexperienced recruits, who found themselves against battle-hardened, highly skilled veterans. Ten of them fell fatally wounded in seconds. The rowers attacked the flanks, one on one, and more of the young soldiers began to fall. Ballista bolts fired from the boat felled one soldier after another. Marcellus and the centurion fought each other, but Marcellus was too fast, and he rammed his sword straight through his opposition. The centurion fell to the ground gasping his last.

Their leader down, and comrades in arms wounded and dying, the remaining soldiers battled on, but Marcellus's smaller force got round the back of them, and their formation began to collapse into a disorganised scrum. Regulus watched, sword in hand ready to defend the boat as the battle raged. Swords stabbed and slashed, ballista bolts zinged through the air, the Arma Officinas soldiers found themselves in a killing zone. The rowers showed tremendous strength and courage as they closed in on the flanks adding more pressure to their enemies. Dadas had two swords, whirling and slashing: a reaping windmill of death.

The Arma Officinas soldiers began to panic. Some threw their weapons to the ground, surrendering in a desperate gesture of self-preservation. Those who fought on in vain began to fall to the ground and find themselves in the afterlife. More soldiers threw their weapons to the ground, arms pointing skyward in the hope of being spared the slaughter of the killing zone until all had given up and surrendered.

Marcellus surveyed the scene and ordered his men to collect the surrendered weapons and marshal the disarmed enemy into a line. Eighty of them had started, thirty-eight were left standing, many in a state of shock at the speed of their defeat and the level of violence visited upon them. Marcellus paraded in front of them, gasping for breath, sweat pouring from him, blood dripping from his sword. Some of the surrendered soldiers were visibly shivering with fear at the sight of such an expert warrior in full fight mode radiating aggression and violence, and most were convinced that slaughter and execution were sure to come.

"Your centurion and leader is dead, which one of you is next in line of command?" demanded Marcellus.

One of the surrendered soldiers stepped forward and bolted to attention.

"I am."

"Do you or do you not surrender command of this settlement to me?"

"I do."

"Good. Now, I want to know which men have colluded with Festus and supplied weapons to our enemies."

"Most are dead, including our centurion, but those five men were in on stealing weapons and falsifying the warehouse inventory. And our centurion had slaves crucified for refusing to co-operate with his schemes."

Marcellus was beside himself with anger.

"Execute those five men now!"

The five soldiers pleaded for mercy in vain. Within a minute, all five were forced to their knees and beheaded.

Marcellus turned to the remaining ashen-faced soldiers.

"Anyone else?"

Silence.

Marcellus turned to the surrendered next in command soldier.

"Give me your name."

"Marcus," said the soldier still standing bolt to attention.

"Very well Marcus, see to your wounded and report to me when you're finished. If you or any of your men puts a toe out of place, they will be executed. Understand?"

"Understood Centurion Marcellus," said Marcus as he saluted.

Marcellus walked up the short path to the settlement square and the warehouse. Slaves and villagers cowered as he walked past, terrified by the fighting and what might be in store for them with the arrival and takeover by this force from Bremetenn. But Marcellus had his mind on more pressing matters. He knew he must secure the Arma Officinas with adequate defences as soon as possible to fend off an attack by the Setantii or treacherous Romans loyal to Festus. Sextus had ordered him to hold until relief arrived, and his soldiers would need all the catapults and ballista machines they could pull from the warehouse and get into position. Marcellus knew how effective a small well-disciplined force with artillery could be, and could hold out against a much larger force, especially if the opposition was trying to cross a river.

Inside the warehouse, he took stock of the war machines. He had to smile – Festus had stocked the place to the rafters in anticipation of using the weapons for his enterprise. Now, the settlement, warehouse, and more soldiers were under his command and for the first time he began to feel a little less pessimistic about the chances of success. Lost for a moment in his own thoughts, he was interrupted by Marcus, who came running into the warehouse.

"Smoke is rising on the horizon from the direction of the Hill Fort," gasped Marcus.

"Assemble all the soldiers and slaves in the square."

Marcus ran off to carry out the order. Marcellus went outside and waited for the soldiers and slaves to form up and receive his orders. Things were moving fast, and he knew he must get everything in position before the low tide ford became accessible and with it, passage on foot over the river on the cobbled road. He whispered a short prayer to Mars, for Decimus and Roman victory. The soldiers and slaves fell into line in front of him, waiting for orders; soldiers stood at attention, and slaves stood with their heads bowed low.

"Soldiers of Rome," he began, "place all the catapults to aim at the low tide ford. I want ballista machines along the shoreline on either side of the road, all soldiers armed with bows and as many arrows as you can carry. Regulus, make sure there are plenty of arrows for the ballista machines. Slaves, get to carrying catapult ammunition down to the riverbank. Dismissed!"

Soldiers and slaves saluted, filed into the warehouse, and began the laborious task of carrying and setting up the machines of war, preparing to rain death and destruction on any force bold enough to attack. Civilian men in the settlement came to help hauling the cumbersome catapults from the warehouse to the riverbank. Women civilians and slaves helped the wounded from the recent battle into their homes to recover, and a surgeon stitched one slash and stab wound after another. Two slaves down by the river hastily constructed a funeral pyre and began the grim task of piling on the dead, ready for burning.

Across the river on the opposite bank, a group of Setantii warriors had gathered, pointing, and gesticulating at all the activity as the Romans dug in and added more war machines to the formidable artillery being assembled. The outgoing tide flowed faster and the water level of the Belisama dropped lower. Marcellus guessed that more Setantii would come to reinforce them and mount an attack at low tide.

Slaves sweated under the back-breaking weight of boulders, which they carried down to the catapults from the warehouse. Hay balls soaked in oil were stacked around the catapults ready to be ignited and fired at the enemy to create maximum panic and injury. The Romans worked with relentless energy, digging in pointed wooden stakes along the top of the riverbank and even helping the slaves with labour intensive carrying. The sense of urgency increased as mid-day and low tide approached. If the Setantii were going to mount an attack, it would come very soon. Victory would be dependent upon solid preparation and Marcellus was immersed in the labour, urging the men on, and leading by example.

Onboard the *Belisama Cygnus*, Regulus and the rowers had restocked the ballista machines with bolts and iron balls from the warehouse and placed buckets of water around the boat to extinguish any fires started in a battle. The rowers had armed themselves to the teeth and now they wore helmets and chain mail, which they had plundered from the warehouse. Marcellus had ordered them to stay onboard the boat and defend it to the death. Regulus was satisfied they had done everything they could to defend the boat against an attack he felt sure would come.

More Setantii had gathered on the opposite bank, numbering two hundred at least. Still, they stayed out of range and Marcellus tried to make out who was leading them, and if they were beginning to form up for an attack. They seemed cautious and disorganised, and there did not seem to be anybody in charge. The Romans, on the other hand, were in position and ready with the war machines primed and loaded, each soldier ready to act on Marcellus's order. Tension crackled in the air like static before a lightning strike.

Marcus walked over to Marcellus.

"Centurion, they don't seem to have anyone leading them."

"I know Marcus, it's like they're waiting for someone to give an order."

"Perhaps they are, or they're just worried about what we have waiting for them if they charge."

"Possibly, but we're ready if they try anything."

"At least we'll die an honourable death if we fail."

"You didn't much respect your now deceased centurion, did you?"

"No! I knew he was corrupt, but what can an oath bound soldier of Rome do, but follow orders?"

"I know, to follow orders unto death."

"True. I'll see you in the afterlife."

"There is wine in the warehouse should we prevail. Mars protect you brother."

"I'll drink to that."

Their soldier's banter was interrupted by a blood-curdling battle cry from across the river. Setantii warriors gathered into a loose formation, and charged down the cobbled ford road, two hundred strong, rushing towards the roman position. They clanged their swords and battle axes on their shields chanting in tempo, trying to intimidate their enemy. The Romans pulled their bows taut ready for Marcellus's command, which came as the Setantii reached the middle of the riverbed, the lowest part of the ford crossing.

Marcellus shouted the order at the top of his voice.

"Fire!"

Bows, ballista machines, and catapults launched their lethal payloads: arrows, bolts, iron balls, boulders, and burning balls of oil-soaked hay balls rained down on the charging Setantii. The effect was devasting. Almost half of the Setantii number fell to the ground, wounded and dying. Those at the back of the charge trampled over their comrades-in-arms in a frantic attempt to keep the momentum going and reach the Roman position before the artillery could be reloaded. They were too late.

Marcellus was unrelenting.

"Reload, fire!"

Another volley of artillery rained death and mayhem on the charging Setantii and more lay wounded and dying on the ford road. The rest turned and fled in a desperate attempt to retreat and get out range of the artillery. The ill-conceived attack was bad enough, but what came next surprised the Setantii and the Romans. A small group of cavalry, forty in number, came charging down the road straight into the retreating Setantii warriors. Regulus could not believe his eyes. It was Decimus leading the charge, which smashed through the retreating Setantii warriors, and galloped across the ford, slashing, and stabbing with their long cavalry swords, thundering along the cobbled ford road until they reached the Roman position, where they dismounted, safe behind the Roman defences and artillery line.

In yet another cruel twist for the Setantii wounded on the ford road, the tide had begun to turn and flood into the river. Those who tried to stand and reach safety were cut down one by one by the deadly accuracy and power of the ballista machines. Others tried to crawl only to meet the same fate aided by sharp-shooter archers. For the Romans, victory, at least for now, was sweet. The Setantii had suffered a terrible defeat and the stench of death hung heavy in the air.

The Romans wondered how Decimus and some of the Hill Fort cavalry had managed to battle their way through the roadblocks and ambushes. They had assumed that the Hill Fort had been taken by the Setantii warriors of the Fylde area. However, Decimus had a different story to tell. Marcellus rushed over to Decimus so each could report and plan the next moves in defence of the Arma Officinas.

"Primus Pilus Decimus, welcome," said Marcellus.

"Centurion Marcellus, I thank you, let us report."

"We have secured Arma Officinas as ordered by Prefect Sextus. All traitors are dead including their centurion."

"Excellent. I come from the Hill Fort, which is now a burned ruin. The Setantii attacked this morning in their thousands. We could not hold against such numbers, so I followed Prefect Sextus's orders and set fire to the fort to render it useless to the enemy. Then we charged out of the fort and headed along the road to reach the low tide ford and help in the securing of Arma Officinas. We lost over half our number along the way, including the Hill Fort captain, but, as you can see, forty of us have made it through the ambushes. I saw Festus on his horse heading away in the direction of the Trough Valley."

"We must hold this position to the last man, and, if necessary, burn the warehouse to the ground. We can't let Festus get his hands on all this artillery, or Bremetenn is doomed," added Marcellus.

"In that we are as one," Decimus replied.

Marcus walked over to the two of them.

"Primus Pilus, centurion, I know of something that might be of some use."

"Go on," said Marcellus.

"There is a young slave boy in the settlement who keeps pigeons.

Marcellus and Decimus looked at each other and looked at Marcus as if he had gone mad.

"This is hardly the time for tavern stories," said Marcellus.

"No, I'm serious. Some of them are from Bremetenn. If released, the pigeon will fly home. We can attach a message to bring Sextus up to date."

Decimus looked unimpressed.

"I've seen pigeons used before during my years of action with the Legio XX – unreliable and a liability if they fall into enemy hands. Much better on the dining table."

Marcellus was more optimistic.

"But it might work, so let's at least give it a try."

"On your heads be it," sighed Decimus, "stupid birds!"

Marcellus wrote the message on a small piece of parchment and went with Marcus to the house where the young slave boy lived and served. The slaves and citizens were still terrified after the bloodshed and violence, and none more so than the ten-year-old slave boy who kept the pigeons. Marcus ordered him to select the bird from Bremetenn in the hope that it would fly home once released. The boy attached the message to the pigeon's leg and released it from captivity. The bird took to the air and flapped away in the wrong direction, heading west instead of east. Marcellus looked at

Marcus, inhaled, puffed out his cheeks, and deflated very slowly. Marcus could barely contain himself at the look of sheer disbelief and consternation on the poor boy's face.

"Best not tell Decimus," said Marcellus.

"Let's get some of that wine we promised ourselves," added Marcus, and they both trudged off to the warehouse.

Regulus was busy on the boat, double checking everything so it would be ready to sail at a moment's notice. He was still shaken by the level of violence and bloodshed, which he had never witnessed before. It was one thing to read about famous Roman battles and victorious legions, and quite another to be in the thick of such brutality. He knew how to handle a sword, but he was sensible enough to know that he was average at best and any skilled warrior would better him in seconds. His thoughts were interrupted by Decimus on the jetty walking towards him.

"It's good to see you alive Decimus," said Regulus forgetting the usual formalities.

"And you," replied Decimus, "I didn't think either of us would survive our missions."

"Yet here we are, but I do have some bad news."

"Let me guess, Gabo."

"Yes. We held the funeral according to his wishes before we left."

"He didn't look good when I saw him. He will be celebrated and welcome in the afterlife."

"He will, and Festus will pay for his murderous treachery."

"All in good time. First, we must hold our position – there are thousands of Setantii out there in the marshes."

"So we do what we can until relief comes."

"Nothing less. What happened to that impudent little slave woman?"

"Sabina is in Bremetenn. We both made it back from the mission."

Decimus nodded a half-approval.

"She's got some cahonis, I'll give her that."

The Romans busied themselves setting up tents, braziers and campfires along the riverbank and organising four hours on, four hours off watches. Decimus and Marcellus arranged opposite watches, grateful of each other's capability to take command, with Marcus serving as a useful second. Decimus had not slept since Sabina's dramatic arrival in Bremetenn, and he ached from head to foot from lack of sleep. He had refused to rest or sleep at the Hill Fort, standing stoically on the ramparts watching for any movements that might signal an attack from the Setantii.

When the Setantii did attack, they came in their thousands, creeping up the hillside and rowing their canoes and coracles along the waterways of the estuary and the Fylde. Decimus had given the order to burn the Hill Fort, mount the horses, and charge out onto the road in the direction of Arma Officinas. Many had died in the fighting along the way, including the Hill Fort captain.

So Decimus sat down next to a campfire to rest and eat. A slave brought him some bread, cheese, and olives along with a cup of wine. As he ate, he gazed into the flames of the fire, grateful for food, warmth, and the pain numbing effect of the wine. He began to drift off to sleep as muddled thoughts ran through his mind - thoughts of fallen brothers-in-arms and the cries of the wounded and dying. Then his memory switched to Bremetenn, his home for the last fifteen years. He longed to be there, breeding horses, working the land, and chiselling the stones to reconstruct the wooden ramparts and parapets of the fort. He longed to build and farm, not to be out here fighting like his younger days with the Legio XX.

Strange it was that he recalled his arrival at Bremetenn when he fell for a young slave woman, and the three-month romance that followed before she ended it. Then he fell into a deep sleep, lulled by the sweet memories of those all too brief idyllic days of summer romance.

Chapter Six
Something about Sabina

There was something about Sabina that Lyra could not quite place, and it irked and attracted her at the same time. She knew she was feisty wild independent and quick to learn, but she could not reason away the notion that she was born to lead. That, for Lyra, did not add up. She viewed Sabina as a young naïve slave woman; a slave from the moment she was born and as they watched the *Belisama Cygnus* sail away, her arm around Sabina's shoulders and Sabina's arm around her waist, she knew Sabina was attracted to her. In that knowledge, she was sure, but she resolved to probe deeper, and find out what this natural talent was that she sensed so compellingly.

The two of them walked back to Lyra's apartment and prepared to settle in to get some sleep. Sabina put two cushions on the floor and pulled a woollen blanket over herself. Despite Lyra's offer of a spare bed, she could not get used to the comfort after the rough life in the slave shed at Portus Piscium, and would still awaken in the night and go outside to look at the moon and stars, loving the feel of the cold night air flowing through her untamed hair. Lyra reasoned that all slaves, herself included, had suffered, and each had their own way of dealing with past traumas. But there was also the peculiar fact that once Sabina had settled, Dido would stroll over and curl up next to her, purring with contentment. All visitors before Sabina had been ignored and got at best, a supercilious look. Lyra began to wonder if the cat knew more that she did.

They managed some sleep before the light of the sun streaming through the window woke Sabina. She had begun to learn where things were in the apartment, and she pottered about making breakfast. She had also learned that Lyra was most particular about her meals to the last detail: bread cut just so, milk warmed to the correct temperature, and the modest pieces of cheese and salmon had to be the correct size. Then there was the strict table manners, which included eating at a slow pace. According to Lyra, this was good for the digestive system and an excellent way of avoiding embarrassing wind at dinner parties. Even the Dido's scraps had to be laid out in an orderly fashion. Sabina began to think she had a lot to put up with, half-wondering if she preferred the rough and tumble of life out on the marshes to all this, "everything just so".

After breakfast, Lyra announced that it was women's morning over at the bath house, and that they should make their way over at once. Sabina could not help feeling a rush of excitement at the prospect of being with Lyra in the bath house again, although she knew they would not be alone this time. She muttered to herself about everything having to be done in a certain way at a certain time, a little irritated at the regimentation of it all, but again she held back and set about doing things the Roman way.

The early morning dank and drizzle had given way to some bright sunshine as they walked along the riverbank, past the fort towards the bath house. The first leaves of spring had begun to show more in all their bright green freshness and the sky was alive with birdsong. The clear water of the Belisama glistened, random jewels showing and hiding in the ceaseless flow. Not for the first time did Sabina compare the beauty of the river at Bremetenn to the drab brown water at Portus Piscium. She wanted to stop and admire with wonder, but Lyra strode on with purpose, leading her to the bath house and the changing room door. They entered, removed all clothing, and padded into the Sudatorium, the sweating room. It was full of women from Bremetenn: some slaves given leave to bathe, Romanised Brigante, Freedwomen, and the bath house slave women led by Astrid.

Lyra began to teach Sabina the Latin names for things, such as the paraphernalia used for bathing as they sat sweating and applying the cleansing oil over their bodies, scrapping off the dirt with a strigil. They followed this process with a luxuriant soak in a hot pool. Sabina was careful to remember all she could about what Astrid had shown her on that first visit after the escape.

Having bathed and cleansed their skin and hair, they made their way to the Caldarium, the hot room, and made themselves comfortable. Sabina wondered at the ingenuity of providing heat from underneath the tiled floor and Lyra explained how a pyrocaust diverted heat from the furnace. For everything Lyra explained, Sabina had more questions, curious and inquiring, wanting to know and understand more. Lyra was only too happy to play tutor to such an inquisitive student, enjoying the challenge of Sabina wanting to take things further than rote naming and spelling.

Finally, they walked through to the Tepidarium, the warm room where there was a good deal of chattering and gossiping about life in the village and the "goings on" plus the routine outrage about, "the price of olive oil". Then they plunged into the icy grip of the cold-water plunge pool, which took Sabina's breath away, as Lyra became ever more expansive about the skin pores closing and finishing the bathing process. They went to dress and once again Lyra helped Sabina style her hair in the Roman fashion. Sabina began to realise her good fortune at being taken under the wing of such a capable tutor and finally having access to at least some form of education. That, if for no other reason, made the risk of escaping the clutches of Stultus and Festus worthwhile.

"And now we must visit Seren to get you measured for a linen tunic," said Lyra, breaking off from her tutor role.

Sabina was taken aback.

"For me?"

"Ah, yes. I can't have you following me around in that boring grey tunic all the time.

"I've never owned such a thing in my life!"

Lyra laughed, "I'll make a Roman of you yet!"

"I've no doubt you will, but I'm still a lowly slave and still owned by Festus."

"Have faith Sabina, things can change fast in this world, and I've told you I have an idea," said Lyra not without a hint of impatience.

Sabina bowed her head.

"I shall follow your lead."

They left the bath house, walked back along the riverbank to the fort, and began to work their way up the gravelled road to Seren's apartment. Along the way, the market bustled with activity, life going on as normal, oblivious to the fights taking place at the Hill Fort and Arma Officinas. Sabina followed behind as Lyra bought supplies from the baker and the butcher, finishing off at the stall selling olive oil and wine, and continuing up the road to Seren's apartment and stall.

Seren hugged them both when they arrived as they inquired after her welfare, knowing how worried she must be about her son participating in such a dangerous mission.

"I'm so delighted to see you both," said Seren.

"How are you?" said Sabina.

"One step at a time and being patient for news about Regulus."

"The Romans will prevail," said Lyra confidently.

"I pray to all the gods you are right," Seren whispered.

They all hugged again before Lyra got down to business.

"Now, I'd like you to measure Sabina for a linen tunic."

"It would be my pleasure," said Seren and she produced a measuring tape as if by magic.

Sabina stood still as Seren and Lyra fussed around her, Lyra insisting that the tunic should fit a certain way here and there as Seren made careful notes as she went along. Sabina became impatient with all the bustle, only to be reproached by Lyra and told to stop fidgeting. Then there was uproar a few doors down at the baker's stall. A young boy had been caught red-handed stealing a meat pie, and the baker had hold of the boy, shouting at him while the boy's mother remonstrated at him to get his hands off her son while alternately scolding the boy for stealing.

Lyra broke off from the tunic fitting session and went to pay the baker for the pie, hoping to shut them up. As she did so, another boy sneaked around the back and pinched another meat pie from the stall. Sabina stifled her laughter at such brazen cheek as he scuttled off undetected to enjoy his ill-gotten gain, while the baker and the other boy's mother were pacified by Lyra's intervention. If it had been a classic distraction set-up, things could not have gone better.

The measuring and fussing about started again and Seren assured Lyra that the tunic would be ready soon and she would call at the apartment for final fitting. Again they all hugged and said a prayer for Regulus's safe return and deliverance from violence for Bremetenn. Lyra and Sabina set off back down the road to the apartment, calling at the fort on the way where Lyra asked one of the guards for an audience with Sextus.

At the apartment, Lyra began to prepare the main meal of the day and set about instructing Sabina in the formal Roman way of setting the table between two recliner couches. Each type of food had to be in separate bowls as she muttered about how anything else was considered barbaric and unacceptable. She pointed to each item and insisted Sabina repeat the Latin words. Everything had to be set according to Lyra's instructions until it all looked like one of the fresco paintings on the wall.

Sabina had never known anything like it. She had heard snippets about how Roman society lived, but this was the first time she had seen it let alone participate.

She started to eat fast, still finding it difficult to break away from slave mode and years of deprivation, but once again Lyra slowed her down, not in a reproachful way but gently reminding her to savour the food and enjoy the whole experience as one of life's pleasures. Sabina struggled not to rush despite her eagerness to learn from Lyra's example.

Lyra, curious as ever, wanted to know more about Sabina's past, especially her early years at Deva.

"Who was your master at Deva?" she asked.

"He was a very old, retired centurion from the Legio XX."

"What duties did you perform for your master?"

"Hmm, most of the time I was with the other girls and women slaves helping to cook and serve food to the soldiers in the barrack's canteen. My master always ate in the canteen because he loved being with the other soldiers."

"How were you treated?"

"Well compared to some. Many of the soldiers liked me being around – hmm, they missed their wives and children, but others were brutes who wanted to fight all the time."

"Did you ever know your mother?"

"No, my master told me she died soon after giving birth to me."

"I notice you have some basic numeracy and literacy skills. How did you learn?"

"My master used to teach me a few things," said Sabina modestly, "and some of the kinder soldiers did too. I picked things up around Deva, but not so much at Portus Piscium."

"How did you end up at Portus Piscium?"

"I don't remember much, but one day a slave trader told me to go with Festus, my new master, and that was that. I was heart-broken because my old master was the only family I had ever known. And Deva was a nicer place than the marshes and that dreadful slave shed."

"Do you remember your old master agreeing to the sale?"

"No, well…" Sabina trailed off, "I was only seven – I think – and all the people I'd ever known were in Deva. I shut everything out and tried to survive from one day to the next. It was a living nightmare. So many slaves died in that filthy shed: fevers, accidents, some from being flogged by Stultus, the monstrous slave driver, and one by crucifixion for trying to escape three times."

"Try to remember if there was a formal slave sale."

"I DON'T KNOW!" shouted Sabina becoming very agitated and distressed.

Lyra pulled back since it was clear to her that evoking memories of those years was traumatic for Sabina. She remembered the horrors of her own sale in Antioch as a small child and having no memory of her journey on the Silk Road. She sat next to Sabina and put her arms around her in a comforting embrace.

"I'm sorry, I didn't mean to upset you," she said in her softest honey voice.

"I'm sorry I can't be more helpful, because I had to survive and push those memories away."

"I understand, but if we could find your old master, we may discover that Festus acquired you through illegal means. Slave theft and piracy are rife throughout the empire."

"Really?"

"Yes, really, despite severe penalties for those who get caught."

"I didn't know it was so frequent."

Lyra began to tell Sabina about her own sale in Antioch and how the memory had stalked her with feverish nightmares. Then there was the upset of being sold again after Marius had been made bankrupt. Sabina listened as they embraced each other, brought together by the injustices of being owned, albeit with quite different experiences. While Sabina had ached for Lyra on a physical level, it was enough, for now, to be comforted. Lyra began to be clearer about Sabina and the possibility that she had been abducted and sold to Festus, or perhaps he had arranged things himself.

A knock on the door interrupted their quiet conversation. Lyra opened the door, and a guard told her to go for an audience with Sextus. Sabina began to clear things away as Lyra slipped on her cloak and followed the guard over to Sextus's quarters. She arrived to find him looking very tired and sleep deprived as she greeted him in a formal way, careful to maintain her disarming charm and poise. Sextus offered her a seat.

"You asked to see me," said Sextus, his voice weary and hoarse.

"Yes, I have an idea of how to deal with Festus."

"Very well, what do you have in mind?"

"Festus is greedy for one thing: money."

"I know this. And?"

"Simple. You arrange a meeting under a flag of truce. I will arrange a bribe and an escape route out of Britannia."

"What makes you think he'll find that acceptable?"

"Because he knows he can't win."

"I wouldn't be so sure. We don't have enough information to make that assumption."

"You know the tribes will not hold together. Rome has won so many campaigns with that knowledge: divide, conquer, and rule."

"True, but I still need to know that the Legio XX are on the way. Negotiations need to be backed up by military muscle and steel."

"You've had no word?"

"No. For all I know all the runners have been caught and the Hill Fort and Arma Officinas are in Festus's hands."

"I see."

"All that said, we can wait until news does come through, and then we could discuss your scheme."

"I shall wait to hear from you."

"Oh, can I assume you would arrange a double cross for Festus?"

Lyra gave him her most innocent look.

"What makes you think I would come up with such a thing?"

Sextus gave her a bleak smile.

"We shall speak later. Now I must get on with things."

Lyra left and walked back to the apartment, deep in thought and concerned about the precariousness of the situation at Bremetenn. Courage in the face of violence was not one of her strong points and she was fearful of what might be in store if the Romans were defeated and Bremetenn fell into the hands of Festus and the Brigante warriors. Slaughter, rape, and slavery would surely follow. On the other hand, if the Legio XX arrived soon, she knew it would be almost certain defeat for the Festus and his rebel army.

As she entered the apartment, Sabina greeted her with a hug and she responded, putting her arms around Sabina, who could sense that Lyra was not quiet her usual confident self. Sabina gave her a gentle kiss on the cheek. Lyra leaned back and they looked into each other's eyes; Sabina into Lyra's deep pools of soft brown and Lyra into Sabina's flashing emeralds. In that briefest of moments, they knew. Sabina gave Lyra a deep kiss on her lips, and they locked together in a passionate embrace. Lyra leaned back again and lowered her voice to a soft whisper.

"Come to bed lover."

Sabina nodded and followed Lyra to the main bedroom. They embraced again and began removing each other's clothing, kissing between each item until they stood naked and fell on the bed. Sabina began to kiss and caress Lyra's voluptuous curves as Lyra pulled her closer, guiding her hands and whispering words of passion, her breathing becoming deeper and faster as Sabina responded.

Then Lyra began to kiss and caress Sabina, slow and gentle to start with and steadily becoming firmer. Sabina was quick to climax, climbing higher and higher as Lyra's experience left her gasping for breath. Lyra nestled in beside her, wrapping her arms and legs around her and softly stroking her head as they slipped away into a contented sleep.

Sabina was woken by Dido, who had decided to start biting her left big toe, demanding attention. Lyra was still asleep, arms and legs around her, which felt divine, so she was loathe to move. She gave the cat a shove with her foot, which only served to encourage it into full playtime mode. She decided to wake Lyra, who released her from the soft and warm embrace.

"I didn't want to wake you, but Dido will not leave me alone," said Sabina.

"Ah, she can be a bit of a nuisance at times," she said as she rose, grabbed the cat, and put it outside the bedroom, closing the door behind her.

She came back to bed and laid next to Sabina.

"Did you enjoy our little session?"

"It was gorgeous,"

"I did too, it was lovely."

"Do many women have sex with each other?" asked Sabina, curious and wide-eyed.

"Many more than you might suppose."

"What about husbands and boyfriends?"

"Oh they still have those, but, well, it's just sex for the pleasure of it. Some women prefer women, some men prefer men, and many, well, like both."

"Hmm, I thought marriage was a sacred thing."

"On the surface, it is. Behind closed doors, it's a different matter. Slaves and citizens are barred from marriage, soldiers spend years away from their wives and families, hundreds of miles away from home. Take Astrid and Marcellus for example."

"What about them?"

"They've been lovers for ten years. Marcellus's home is in Spain, and he's been posted here all that time."

"They're an unlikely couple. Astrid is twice Marcellus's size."

"Opposites often attract and besides, Astrid is an excellent lover."

"How do you know – oh, wait, don't tell me."

"Ah, you see, and you wouldn't believe some of the affairs that go on."

"You seem to know all about them."

"I do indeed. In fact, I make it my business to know. We women have so little power in the mighty machine that is the Roman Empire, but knowing what goes on underneath the veneer is power."

Sabina paused for thought to digest what Lyra had told her. Much of what she had assumed crumbled before Lyra's matter-of-fact view of life and civilisation in the world that was Rome. It seemed many things were steeped in a good deal of hypocrisy. She thought about things in the context of her fledgling romance with Regulus and how they would always be barred from marriage if she remained a slave. Perhaps the only happiness slaves could have would always be a secret, hidden away from prying official eyes and ears.

She wondered if Lyra had ever found happiness.

"Have you ever been in love?"

"I thought I was for a while – one of the young slave men at Marius's villa. As things turned out, he decided he didn't much like women."

"What did he like."

"Do keep up."

"Oh, I see."

"In any case, why have just the one lover when there's so much to choice to be had?"

"I suppose…"

"Anyway, it's mid-afternoon. We had better get dressed."

"What about us?"

"It was lovely. It might happen again, or it might not."

Sabina felt confused and hurt by Lyra's dismissive attitude, but she pushed her emotions back. If, as Lyra had explained, knowledge was power, then she wanted more of it and, as things stood, Lyra was the key to more knowledge.

✠✠✠✠✠✠✠✠

Sextus was deep in thought about his next move. It was clear to him that he needed more information about the situation at the Hill Fort and Arma Officinas so, at least for now, he put that out of his mind. Most troubling was the report about the Brigante army gathered in the Trough Valley. He had discussed the possibility of a surprise attack with his centurions, but they had all concluded that being outnumbered eight to one was not a risk worth taking. Hit and run cavalry tactics would be constrained by the cramped space and terrain of the valley, so that was not an option.

In the end, all had concluded that a firm defence of the fort was the best option in the present circumstances. The road to the fort was narrow with the village buildings on either side and the double ditches defence with the river at the back of them would limit how many warriors could attack at any one time. Reducing the odds would give the Romans a better fighting chance with the possibility of a cavalry counterattack. Festus and the Brigantes might then be forced to negotiate a truce and give Lyra an opportunity to bring her bribe plan into play.

If, however, word had reached Deva and the Legio XX mobilised, they would be at Bremetenn within two days, or a day if they marched through the night. The combined force of the legion and his Austurian Cavalry would overwhelm the Brigante army. The Setantii would be no match for them either. It was all very well if things happened that way, but in the short term, Bremetenn stood alone. He decided he needed some fresh air to try and relieve a thumping headache. As he walked to the south gate of the fort, and the bridge over the Belisama, soldiers on guard saluted as he walked past. As he reached the south gate, he noticed one of his centurions was taking his turn on guard.

Sextus turned and addressed the centurion.

"How goes your day?"

"Well sir, and you?"

"Good enough, how are the men?"

The centurion was surprised by the sudden informal address.

"You make speak freely."

"They are all in good form. Most want to get on with fighting the Brigante rebels. All of them want to be the one to capture Festus."

Sextus smiled, "Tell them I'm determined to beat them to it!"

The centurion laughed, "And me, sir."

"Good men, you and all."

"Thank you, sir, we know you will lead us to victory."

They saluted each other and Sextus walked to middle of the bridge, watching the river flow. He felt refreshed by the fresh spring air and cool breeze. In that moment, he thought of Lyra and how much he would like to see her on one of her informal visits to his quarters. Of course, that would have to wait. He strolled, at a slow pace, back to the south gate, whispering a prayer that news would come sooner rather than later.

His thoughts were interrupted by the frantic clanging of the alarm bell, and he ran into the fort square to be met by one of the scouts as soldiers scrambled to muster stations, the centurions barking orders.

Sextus was abrupt, "Report."

"Sir," the scout paused for breath, "Prefect Sextus, the Brigante army are marching towards Bremetenn."

"Where are they and how many?"

"They are at the three-mile mark, marching at a fast pace. Four thousand at least and maybe more in the hills. They will be here within the hour – at least, well, that's my best estimate."

"And Festus?"

"Leading the main column on the road with a Brigante chief."

"Good. Refresh yourself quickly and report to your cavalry centurion."

"Sir!"

Sextus mounted a three feet high wooden platform in front of the assembled soldiers to give final orders and prepare for a battle.

"Centurions, soldiers of Rome, you have your orders. Form up and prepare to defend Bremetenn with your lives. Mars protect you and make this our finest hour."

Every soldier raised their sword in the air and bellowed, "Hail Ceasar" with all their might.

Sextus went to dress for battle as the villagers poured into the fort to take refuge in the soldier's barracks.

Chapter Seven

Crushed

The Brigante chief and Festus led the marching army on the final three miles of road towards Bremetenn having linked up together in the Trough Valley. Festus road his horse in full Roman battle armour, excited about taking the fort and village, and with it, control of the Belisama and all roads north. He was also looking forward to supervising a battle once more after years of dull monotonous life at Portus Piscium. It felt good to have some action back in his life. Nothing like the adrenalin rush of a battle in the theatre of war.

He had overseen the attack on the Hill Fort earlier that day, but he remained disinterested in the outcome as he considered the Setantii tribe mere sword fodder to distract the Romans and keep them occupied in the marshes. The forts and roads were key to gaining control of the territory, which was, of course, why the Romans had set things up that way in the first place with fast transport and movement of military capability.

As the army moved closer to Bremetenn, one of the Brigante outriders came galloping towards them and went straight to Festus to report.

"Sir, the Romans have abandoned Bremetenn."

"Explain!"

"There's not a soul to be seen. I got within a hundred yards of the north end of the village. Nothing."

The Brigante chief was triumphal.

"There Festus, I told you they would run rather than face such overwhelming odds."

Festus was cautious.

"Let's not be too hasty. It could be a trap."

They moved along the road until they came to the top of the hill looking down at Bremetenn lying at the bottom of the Belisama valley. What they saw confirmed the outrider report. Not a soul in sight, just a stray dog looking for scraps and a few chickens pecking around. The *Belisama Cygnus* was conspicuous by her absence, and only a thin plume of smoke spirited from the bath house chimney. Festus looked at the woods on the east and west side with some suspicion, looking for signs of movement.

He turned to the Brigante chief.

"We should send scouts to check the woods and inside the fort," he said, cautious as ever.

The Brigante chief sniffed and tossed his long shoulder length black hair.

"We should seize the opportunity and move in now before nightfall."

"Listen to me, it will not take long to check the woods and then we can move forward."

The Brigante chief was contemptuous.

"We have waited long enough for this moment. Wait here if you want, but I'm moving my warriors in. So what if there are Romans around. We'll fight them and beat them."

Festus lost his temper.

"Can't you see this could well be a trap?"

The Brigante chief ignored him and shouted the order.

"MARCH!"

The column moved forward with the Brigante chief at the head, swords and axes drawn, shields up. They marched down the road and into the village, more warriors following behind filling up the village and moving forward towards the north gate of the fort. The Brigante chief noticed that the doors in the gate archway were partially open, and the parapets were unmanned. No guards, no soldiers, no villagers, and ripe for the taking.

When they were twenty yards from the north gate, the Brigante chief called a halt. The order took time to get through to the warriors at the back and the column packed in tighter, surrounded by buildings on the left and right with the fort walls in front of them. The Brigante chief ordered some of the warriors into the fort. As they started to file through the north gate, they saw a lone Roman soldier in the square holding a bell rope. He waved, smiled, and rang the alarm bell with great vigour.

A voice bellowed out of the shadows.

"ATTACK!"

Roman archers, who had crouched down behind the north facing parapet, sprang up above and behind the Brigantes and began firing volleys of arrows down on them. One after another, the Brigantes started to fall. Other Romans, hidden behind the barracks appeared, some running up onto the ramparts with their bows to join the other archers and some attacking the Brigantes, shields up and swords drawn, in a tight formation. Volley after volley of arrows rained down on the

Brigantes. Some tried to turn and leave the fort only to come up against more warriors trying to get in and join the fight. A lethal crush began to develop inside the fort and outside in the cramped space between the village buildings. Some of the Roman archers fired down outside the fort, adding to the rising panic.

Festus stood at the top of the hill watching in despair. He could tell that the chief and his warriors had been caught in the classic trap of constricting a larger enemy force into a cramped killing zone. He mounted his horse and rode to the back of the column, ordering warriors to pull back and give those further forward room to manoeuvre. To no avail. The warriors were all fired up and eager to get to the fort to join their comrades in arms in the fight. Still Festus persisted and tried to get the men to form small groups with spaces in between for a more effective and disciplined assault.

At the front of the column, hundreds of the Brigantes poured out through the small space on the west side of the fort and onto the riverbank, gasping for breath and relieved to be free of the crush. Their relief was short-lived. They had not noticed the rhythmic puffing of smoke from the bath house chimney signalling to the cavalry hidden in the woods. The cavalry charged straight at them, hitting them with a devasting impact, the Romans inflicting blows and stabs with spears and swords, mounted archers firing multiple arrows with deadly accuracy. Some of the Brigantes fought courageously, while others tried to run only to be pushed back into one of the defence ditches, impaled on wooden spikes below. More arrows rained down on them from the fort.

The Roman cavalry reorganised themselves into a tight formation, kettling the Brigantes who tried without success to push against the horses and fight back. Still more Brigantes were pushing to get out from between the village buildings and the crushing effect became ever more lethal for those trapped in the middle. The north gate of the fort became blocked as the dead and the dying piled up, killed by the relentless arrows, Roman swordsmen in the fort, and the suffocating crush. The Brigante chief, who had led the ill-conceived assault, lay dead at the bottom of the pile.

Some of the Brigante warriors had broken into the barracks to be met by some of the more aggressive villagers. The sight of the blacksmith with a lump hammer, Sabina with two long kitchen knives, and Astrid brandishing an iron skillet was enough to strike fear into the bravest. Lyra and Seren crouched down in a corner, arms around each other, terrified by the violence that was unfolding. Mothers held onto their children while the men grabbed anything they could lay their hands on that could be used as a weapon. Every Brigante that came through the door was set upon, and, as with the fort entrance, the dead and injured piled up further restricting assess into the barrack.

Other Brigante warriors had jumped into the river or fled trying to cross the bridge. Those on the bridge presented easy targets for the Roman archers, while some of those in the river were not strong swimmers and drowned, caught out by powerful currents and deep water. More Brigantes were dead, dying, or severely wounded with every minute that passed. Others had run along the riverbank towards the bath house and sanctuary in the woods only to face slave skirmishers, strategically hidden to cut off those who tried to retreat.

Festus was still frantic at the back of the column, urging the warriors to retreat and release the pressure at the front. Gradually, the column began to move back, fighting a desperate battle of survival rather than taking control of Bremetenn. On the west side, the two hundred strong Roman cavalry retreated allowing more Brigantes to spill out from the village death trap, but it was a deliberate tactic. As they retreated, a fresh wave, one hundred and fifty strong charged out of the woods and hit the Brigantes again, blocking the exit and increasing the pressure once more. Again and again, the Romans hit them, merciless with the hit and run tactic.

As word passed down the Brigante column to retreat, the panicked warriors began to run, walk, or crawl back up the road to join Festus and what remained of the army. Four thousand had arrived at Bremetenn. Two thousand were missing, presumed killed in battle, wounded, or taken prisoner. Festus ordered a full retreat to the three-mile mark to take stock and full command, believing that the Brigantes had learned their lesson the hard way and the folly of their chief's failed full-frontal attack. The remaining warriors were shaken by the ferocity and lethal efficiency of the Roman defence and counterattack.

At the fort, the Romans began to check for any remaining Brigante warriors, killing the wounded and herding the few that had surrendered into a group and binding them with chains. Sextus mounted the wooden platform in the fort square, blood pouring from a slash wound on his right arm and another slash wound on his left side. He ordered his centurions to report numbers of Roman dead or wounded, and how many Brigantes had surrendered.

Two hundred yards downstream from the fort, soldiers and slaves began the thankless task of building a huge funeral pyre to dispose of the dead Brigantes. The Roman dead were laid to one side ready for more formal funerals with all rites for their journey into the afterlife. The Brigante prisoners sat chained to each other under guard, watching their fallen comrades in arms being thrown without ceremony into the diabolical fire. They were not optimistic about their own fate, expecting execution or, at best, slavery for the rest of their days.

The villagers were ordered to stay in the barracks for the time being until all homes had been checked for any Brigante warriors that might be hiding, and to assess damage. Lyra and Seren were still shaking with fear. Sabina looked like a ferocious warrior, still holding a bloody kitchen knife from where she had stabbed a Brigante who had tried to attack inside the barrack and harm Lyra. Astrid still had hold of the iron skillet and her usual smiling face was set like concrete in a stern frown of Teutonic determination.

Sextus was with two of his centurions, the three of them still wearing full battle dress.

"Do we have a report on our dead and wounded?" asked Sextus.

"The initial account is thirty-six dead and forty-two wounded. The wounded have been taken to the Infirmary," answered one of the centurions.

Sextus turned to the other centurion.

"Make all proper arrangements for funeral formalities for our fallen brothers-in-arms. I want full dedications."

The centurion saluted and ran off to organise things.

Sextus stood in silence with the other centurion, contemplating his next move. Should he take the initiative and get the men together to hound and harass the remaining Brigante, or stay and defend Bremetenn, hoping the Legio XX would arrive sooner rather than later? He knew another attack would come and with it, the possibility of Brigante reinforcements from across the Pennine Hills. He checked himself, reasoning that he still had to work with the evidentiary fact that Bremetenn stood alone. He further reasoned that a defensive strategy had served him well so far, especially when coupled with a well-planned counterattack.

"Come centurion, let us address the prisoners."

As he arrived at the huddled prisoners, guards kicked them to their feet, shouting at them to stand and bow their heads in the presence of a Roman Prefect.

Sextus looked at them with disdain.

"You treacherous scum," he barked with fury, "we had a treaty of peace between the tribes of Britannia and Rome, and you chose to violate it. Do any of you have anything to say in your defence?"

One of the Brigante warriors raised his head.

"We are sick of your treaties. You enslave us, we die young doing your back-breaking work on the roads, choking down your dangerous mines, and crippled in stone quarries. You murder and crucify anyone with the courage to stand against these injustices and the corrupting influence of Rome. And for this you have the audacity to call us barbarians. To Hades with you and your hypocritical cack!"

Sextus was livid.

"How dare you barbarian, and what cack you speak. The tribes to the south of the Belisama live Romanised lives in peace and prosperity."

"Because they haven't got the spine to stand up for themselves, that's why," stormed the Brigante with vitriolic menace.

Sextus addressed the soldiers.

"Bring them," and he led the way up the road and out of the village to open ground.

The sun was low on the western skyline and an icy wind blew across the Pennine moors, causing the prisoners to shiver as they faced what they guessed were their final moments of life. The warrior who had exchanged words with Sextus stood erect, tall, and proud, long black hair flowing in the wind, refusing to bow his head as he looked down the valley of the Belisama; the valley where he had run wild as a child and hunted as a man with his brothers.

Then he turned to Sextus.

"So here's your civilisation. This is why we won't bow down when you treat prisoners of war this way. You rape our homeland, destroy our sacred groves, try to break our spirits, and vandalise our bodies. Were's your Pax Romana, your so called 'Peace of Rome' now?"

"Broken, because you broke it. Execute them!"

He turned away, leaving the centurion and his soldiers to carry on with the executions, and walked down the road towards the fort. He decided to visit the Infirmary to check on the wounded. The surgeon was frantic as he ran around, trying to assess which soldiers stood a chance of survival. There was not enough opium to go round, and some were in great pain, pleading for some comfort and relief. The floor was slippery with blood and the surgeon looked more like someone working in an abattoir than in a hospital.

Sextus was still boiling with anger about what he saw as an unnecessary act of violence by Festus and the Brigantes. For Sextus, the world was Rome: clean water, transport, commerce, literature, art, architecture, education – on and on went the list. It was beyond his comprehension that the Brigantes would rather exchange a life of comfort and civility for war and death. He went about the Infirmary doing his best to offer words of comfort and encouragement to the dying soldiers, thanking them for their courage and playing their part in saving Bremetenn from falling into the hands of a treacherous Roman and a barbarian horde. He assured them that they would be avenged when the Legio XX arrived to take the fight to the enemy and the other rebellious tribes of northern Britannia. As he left to go and check on the defences of Bremetenn, he asked the surgeon to try and give as much pain relief to the suffering as possible, assuring him there would be more supplies as soon as could be arranged.

Lyra had insisted that Seren and Astrid would stay at her apartment when they were allowed to leave the barrack. Sabina stood by the window trying to calm down as Astrid bustled about providing water for everyone to wash and drink. Seren and Lyra were still in shock after the violence in the barrack and they exchanged words of comfort. Sabina excused herself since she could not keep still. She ran out of the apartment and down to the loading dock where she splashed water from the river all over herself, scrubbing the blood off her body. The light from the funeral pyre turned the sky crimson and her eyes streamed from the stifling smoke that swirled around. She was furious. She had risked her life to try and avert the horror and slaughter of war, but here it was: the sickening smell of burning bodies, suffering, and unspeakable acts of violence.

A voice from the top of the riverbank interrupted her thoughts.

"Slave, come here."

She turned to see Sextus looking down at her and she ran up the steps, stood in front of him and bowed her head low.

"Yes Prefect Sextus, how can I be of service?"

"Why is your tunic stained with blood?"

"I had to defend Lyra and Seren against one of the Brigante warriors."

"I see. How is Lyra?"

"She is unharmed, but very upset by the bloodshed."

"You seem very angry."

"I am. All this death and burning. This is why I came to warn you in the hope that all this slaughter could be avoided. I am angry with myself for failing."

"Well, at least Festus didn't win and slaughter us."

"True, but sooner or later the legions will be involved, and it will be all out war. Many on both sides will die."

"They will. Nothing can stop it now. I am grateful to you for protecting Lyra."

"It is nothing sir, I merely fulfilled my duty and protected my mistress."

"You should return to her."

"Immediately Prefect Sextus," and she bowed before running back to the apartment.

Despite his dismissive attitude towards Sabina, Sextus could not help admiring her courage and vigour. Strange it was that this escaped slave from a humble outpost in the Belisama estuary marshes had forewarned him of the threat from Festus and his treacherous rebellion, played a vital part in guiding Decimus across the marshes to warn the Hill Fort garrison, and saved Lyra's life. Stranger still that, like Lyra, he was puzzled how she looked and acted like a leader, even with her head bowed with all the solemn respect a simple slave woman would show her master or mistress. His gratitude towards Sabina for saving Lyra's life knew no bounds, because although he and Lyra only met in secret on rare occasions, he was in love with her and had been since he first set eyes on her at the slave market in Marseilles.

That night, all the soldiers at Bremetenn and Arma Officinas were on high alert after a day of attacks by the Brigantes and the Setantii. Sextus faced another sleepless night as he presided over funerals and conferred with his centurions about defences for the following day when he felt sure another attack would come.

Downstream at the Arma Officinas, vigilant soldiers watched for the slightest movement on the opposite bank of the river, and, like their comrades at Bremetenn, felt sure an attack would come with the first light of dawn.

But out on the Watling Street Road to Londinium, to the south of Arma Officinas, something else was stirring. A mighty fast marching column of muscle and steel, six centuries strong with eighty soldiers in each century, was slicing its way through the night. The legendary Legio XX, the Valeria Victrix, was on the march.

Chapter Eight

The 20th Legion: Legio XX

In the darkness of the Londinium Road, torches and lanterns lit the way as six centuries of the Legio XX made their way towards Arma Officinas, hob-nailed boots crunching out a steady rhythm on the gravelled road. Behind them, a procession of oxen and horse drawn wagons loaded with supplies and weapons trundled along keeping pace with the mighty column: slaves, auxiliary soldiers, and women all ready and capable of support duties for the soldiers of the legion.

On the first wagon behind the marching soldiers, sat an old man with hair as white as fresh winter snow on Alpine peaks, and lines in his face that looked like they had been carved by a stone mason's chisel. At eighty-two years of age, he had seen generations of legionaries pass through the twentieth, his old legion, serving and fighting for the Ceasars and the Empire as he once did. He had retired from active service decades ago, but he still lived and breathed the Legio XX. He ate with them, slept with them and wherever they went, he went, to the extent that the soldiers considered it an ill-omen if he was not around. Some considered his presence more important than the boar crest of the legion.

At the front, and leading the cohorts, marched the Primus Pilus, the First Spear Centurion, a man of Syrian origin so muscular that he looked like he had been carved from black granite. Ever vigilant, he had been warned to expect ambushes from the Setantii and Brigantes, and he knew he would be the first to be targeted and the first into action. But he was fierce and fearless. The soldiers were convinced that he was at his happiest when he was engaged in a fight and not one of them would ever doubt his unwavering loyalty to the legion and his courage in battle.

The relentless marching continued, every soldier in the column chosen for their proven stamina to keep going, hour after hour, drinking and eating on the move without rest like marathon runners. The Primus Pilus was determined to keep going to reach Arma Officinas and the ford road across the Belisama by dawn. Once there, he would assess the situation and continue onwards to Bremetenn as ordered by the Legate at Deva. They had received word of the Brigante rebellion from Prefect Sextus via one of his marathon runners and it was apparent that securing Arma Officinas and Bremetenn were of the upmost urgency. All the soldiers knew they would face Brigante warriors, just as they had done when they fought and put down a rebellion four years ago. They were the fastest and most enduring marchers, always first into battle, arriving before the slower cohorts who followed them.

In the distance, the lights from the hotel and baths of Coccium came into view, indicating they had about five hours of marching before reaching Arma Officinas at current pace. On through Coccium they marched, inhabitants of the settlement, woken by the clattering and crunching of the column, came out of their homes to salute and pay tribute to the legendary Legio XX.

The hotel owner was hopeful of a surprise influx of paying guests, only to be disappointed as the column and support wagons passed through and disappeared into the darkness on the other side of town on their unstoppable march. Two hundred yards away, a Brigante ambush party, a hundred strong, could only hide and watch with no possibility of trying to stop the Romans.

At Arma Officinas, Regulus was wide awake on board the boat, eyes darting from left to right as he watched for activity on the opposite side of the river. The boat was his responsibility and he wanted to raise the alarm at the slightest hint of an impending attack by the Setantii. Dadas sat close by, vigilant with his swords drawn ready while the other rowers took turns on four-hour watches.

Regulus turned to Dadas.

"Why don't you get some rest?"

"I can't rest," he said stretching his arms and legs, "I feel another attack will come soon now the ebb tide is lowering the river level."

"I know how you feel…", Regulus tailed off vaguely and added, "if we sleep, we could be caught out and no second chance."

Dadas nodded in agreement.

"We only die once."

"Do you ever feel strange fighting alongside Romans – I mean, we were your enemies at one time."

Dadas raised a wry smile, "Sometimes, when I think of Dacia, my old homeland, and how we gave Emperor Trajan and his legions hell. But we lost, and those days are long gone."

"Do you long to return to Dacia?"

"No. Bremetenn is my home now and I have achieved Freedman's status. Who knows, perhaps one day I will be a citizen and raise a family in Bremetenn."

Regulus sat in thought and spoke in a whisper.

"I too would like to raise a family in Bremetenn."

"Why don't you?" asked Dadas, "you are a free citizen."

"Because the woman I love is a slave. Worse still, she belongs to Festus."

Dadas threw his hands up.

"That's a problem, especially if Festus is declared an enemy of the state. She will be sentenced to death along with all his other slaves."

"I know. I must find some way of buying her before that happens."

"You do, sooner rather than later."

"Sometimes I wonder if there is any justice in this world."

"No justice, just some just people trying to do just things."

"And the law is an ass!"

Marcellus was doing his rounds, checking that all stations were manned and alert. He walked over to were Decimus was camped to find him fast asleep. It would be first light soon, so Marcellus decided to let him rest until then. It was, after all, going to be another long day for Decimus on top of the hard days he had endured without sleep at the Hill Fort. He walked over to Marcus, who stood alert on watch at one of catapults. A slave stood with Marcus, so Marcellus ordered the slave to bring two bowls of porridge.

Both men were surprised at how quickly they had bonded as brothers in arms. They had only just met the day before under circumstances that required them to try and kill each other. But they both recognised something in themselves and in each other: honour, courage, and unshakeable loyalty to Rome and to die in service to the Emperor and the Empire if called upon to do so. It was a bond of brotherhood that would last a lifetime.

Their moment of camaraderie was interrupted by movement over on the opposite side of the river. Starting at a slow pace, five torches were moving towards the shallow water at the centre of the ford. Marcellus was about to give the order to open fire when he saw the flag of truce in the torch light. He sent Marcus to wake Decimus and went to the road on the Roman side of the river. He was distrustful of the truce flag, so he ordered every bow and ballista machine to point at the five Setantii warriors as he beckoned them to come forward. All five Setantii were unarmed.

The lead Setantii warrior was the first to speak.

"Roman, centurion, I come with an offer of peace."

Marcellus looked unimpressed.

"You had peace with our treaty and trade agreements. You broke the Pax Romana, declared war, and now you talk of peace. Do you take us for fools?"

"I speak for the Setantii people. Our elders have led us into conflict with Rome against our wishes."

Marcellus was about to reply when Decimus appeared.

"Marcellus, what's all this about?"

"Looks like they've had enough, and they talk of a truce."

"I'll handle this," said Decimus with authority, as he handed his sword to Marcus.

He strode with confidence to within two paces of the lead warrior.

"What are you offering barbarian?" growled Decimus.

"We want a truce. Our elders have led us into conflict with Rome against the wishes of the Setantii people. The elders have done this to fatten their own purses and have not considered the warriors and people, who well know we can't win a war against Rome and the might of her legions."

Decimus was scathing and contemptuous as he responded to the warrior.

"You're right about one thing – you cannot and will not win. We will fight you to the last man and burn the warehouse to the ground if necessary. The legions will come and turn your Roundhouses to ashes, enslave you, and crucify others to set an example you will not forget."

The Setantii warrior was more conciliatory.

"I'll have our Elders delivered to you along with I and other hostages."

Decimus paused for thought. There was a sincerity and dignity about the warrior. Perhaps this proposal might avoid further bloodshed and losses in the Roman ranks.

"Bring them within the hour and we will talk again."

"I will."

Decimus turned away and walked back to Marcellus.

"They are bringing their Elders and hostages within the hour. Let us see if they are as good as their word. Until then, no change in watch arrangements."

Regulus and Dadas had watched the meeting from the boat, wondering what had been said. They had seen the flag of truce and were hopeful of an end to hostilities. For his own part, Regulus had been surprised that the Setantii had joined the rebellion. In all his voyages with Gabo to the Portus Piscium, the Setantii had always been peaceful and welcoming, enjoying the regular trade with Bremetenn. They were, he thought, a simple people who loved to live their lives close to the sea and the plentiful year-round seafood harvest it brought. To Regulus, it was his hated enemy, Festus Crassus, who had led them to violence with false promises of money and power.

It did not take long for the torches to reappear. Decimus beckoned the lead warrior to come forward along with the two Elders and five other warriors, and they surrendered themselves without condition. Marcus was given the job of placing them under armed guard until Decimus decided what to do next. For now, he was more concerned about what was happening upstream at Bremetenn, and he still had to maintain a constant watch in case the Brigantes launched an attack. The strict day and night four-hour watches had to continue despite the relief of a Setantii surrender.

The tide was now at its lowest ebb and the first glimmer of daylight began to show from behind the Pennine Hills in the east. Decimus began to formulate a plan to retake Portus Piscium with a small force aboard the *Belisama Cygnus*. He walked over to the boat to consult with Regulus about tide timing and whether it would be possible to get into the creek.

"Regulus, will the tide be high enough to take the boat down to Portus Piscium?"

Regulus looked at his tide tabulations.

"It's possible, but the high spring tides are over, so there will only be a short window of time.

"How many men could you take?"

"Hmm, my best estimate is ten at the most."

Decimus turned his head downstream towards the marshes.

"How many Romans does Festus have guarding the port?"

"Usually fifteen plus three slave drivers."

"You say you can get ten men down there?"

"Yes, but it will be tight. If we get stuck on a mudbank, we will be wide open to attack."

Their discussion was interrupted by a rhythmic crunching sound in the distance. They looked at each other, quizzically at first, but as the sound drew nearer, it dawned on them that it was the sound of boots marching in time on gravel. That could only mean one thing: a legion on the move.

Decimus's face lit up and he shouted at the top of his voice.

"By all the gods, it's the twentieth!"

Soldiers cheered and clattered their swords on their shields in time with the marching. Those not on watch rushed to greet the glittering column as it marched through the settlement square and down to the river. Decimus waited at the ford to extend formal greetings since he was in command at Arma Officinas. Regulus left his post on the boat to get a closer look at a legendary legion he had heard so much about, but never seen in his lifetime. He was astounded by block after block of polished steel moving as one and giving off an aura of formidable power.

The Primus Pilus ordered the column to come to a halt and Decimus walked over for formal greetings and report.

"Primus Pilus, you are well met. I am Primus Pilus Decimus, formally of the Legio XX, now on permanent secondment to Prefect Sextus at Bremetennacum. The Setantii have sued for peace, and we have hostages, including their elders. Bremetenn is under threat from a Brigante force over four thousand strong. Arma Officinas is secure. The Hill Fort was fired and abandoned to stop it being used by the Setantii. We plan to retake Portus Piscium with a small force later this morning."

"I thank you Primus Pilus. You are also well met. My orders are to continue onwards to Bremetennacum unless we meet resistance. Since you have secured things here, we will ford the Belisama and march to confront Festus Crassus and his Brigante rebellion. Messenger staging posts have been re-established on the Londinium Road all the way back to Deva. Two more cohorts of the legion are on their way close behind us.

"Good enough. The tide is now low enough for you to ford the Belisama. Mars go with you Primus Pilus."

"And with you Primus Pilus."

They saluted each other and the column moved forward, crossing the river via the ford, auxiliaries and wagons clattering along behind them. Everyone at Arma Officinas saluted and cheered as they went on their way to confront Festus and his Brigante army, feeling the relief of having the twentieth in the locale after the tensions and hostilities of the past twenty-four hours.

Decimus went to confer with Marcellus.

"I am planning to take a ten-soldier force on the boat to take Portus Piscium. You will take charge here."

Marcellus looked downstream and back at Decimus.

"That's a risky one," he said as he paused for thought, "we don't know what might be waiting for you and the tide could leave you trapped."

"The risk is acceptable. Word will fly round that the Legio XX are in the region and that their elders have engaged in peace negotiations."

"I will assume command as ordered," said Marcellus as he saluted.

Decimus walked back to the boat,

"Regulus, how soon can we sail?"

"In three hours when we will have enough water underneath us."

"Good, I shall ready the men."

As the morning wore on, the weather began to close in with a strong south-westerly gale, which brought dark grey clouds laden with rain. The soldiers on watch stood at their posts, stoic against the cold and wet, and with the threat from the Setantii now removed, a soggy malaise set in. One had to be relieved as he had sustained a deep slash wound across his thigh, which was showing signs of infection. Others struggled to keep the fires and braziers going against the interminable wind and rain. There were times when spring in Britannia seemed more like an extension of winter, and this was one of those days. The soldiers who had come down from Bremetenn longed to be back there, perhaps spending a few denarii from their army pay on a hot pastry at the grumpy baker's stall before a good steaming sweat at the bath house.

The last of the carts and auxiliaries forded the river as they trundled along after the column of soldiers and disappeared into the gloom on the Londinium Road. Decimus watched with a strange sense of longing.

He knew they faced a hard fight against the fierce and stubborn Brigantes, but he had spent so many years with the Legio XX, fighting rebellions across the Roman Empire and he regarded them as family to which he would always belong. Then there was that familiar rush of adrenaline that comes before a battle, and the grim camaraderie between brothers-in-arms. It took all his effort to suppress his feelings and stay focused on preparing for the voyage down to Portus Piscium.

The damp grey hours dragged by as the tide turned and began to float the *Belisama Cygnus*. Regulus gave the order for Decimus and his ten hand-picked soldiers to board. They set off against the incoming tide, and although it was approaching the high-water mark, and the current had slowed, it still took all the rowers strength to make progress down towards Portus Piscium. They set the sail too catch the fierce gusting wind, which helped to power them along their way. Regulus steered with care between the marker posts and the soldiers stood five on each side, bows loaded and ready while Decimus manned one of the ballista machines at the front.

There was no sign of any Setantii warriors, and the voyage was uneventful save for the urgency of getting the boat to the creek at Portus Piscium before the tide ebbed away. However, Regulus had calculated well, and they docked alongside the jetty without incident. But there was something unusual about the port. It looked like it had been abandoned. Regulus was astounded. He had never seen the port so devoid of life, and half of him expected to see Sabina running down to the jetty, shadowed by the omnipresent and obnoxious Stultus.

Decimus was on high alert in case it was a trap with the enemy lying in wait to ambush them.

Regulus was finishing off securing the boat when he saw smoke starting to rise from the warehouse chimney.

"Decimus, look," he shouted, pointing up at the warehouse.

Decimus gave an order at once.

"Everyone, draw your swords and follow me."

They formed a loose formation and advanced up the walkway at a slow pace. Decimus led them into the warehouse. An appetising smell wafted from the kitchen area as they entered Festus's dining room. Everything was clean and tidy, and a newly laid fire crackled cheerfully in the fireplace grate. Knives and spoons had been set out on the table. They looked at each other in disbelief. It was as if things had been prepared for high-ranking guests. Then they noticed two girls crouched in a corner, one about ten years old and the other one or two years younger. They looked terrified at the sight of armed soldiers on high alert. Regulus recognised them as the two slaves who always shadowed Sabina. They, in turn, recognised him, ran over, and wrapped their arms around him. He put his hands on the back of their heads, reassuring them, telling them not to be afraid.

Decimus was less than impressed.

"Regulus, these girls are slaves. Take them back to the slave shed where they belong."

"Don't be so harsh, look at how well they have kept things in order and prepared for our arrival."

Decimus went into full Primus Pilus mode.

"How dare you disobey my order. Take them back to the slave shed. Now!"

Regulus lost his temper.

"Or what?" he fumed, "I'm so fed up with the way obedient and honourable slaves are treated. These slaves have shown nothing but loyalty to their posts."

Decimus reached forward, grabbed Regulus by his tunic, and slammed him against the wall.

"Do as you are ordered, or I'll have you flogged," he roared at the top of his voice.

"Go on then," spat Regulus, "do it, you're just like that despicable Stultus. It will not change the fact that I love Sabina and I will not let cruel slave laws stand in my way."

Decimus let Regulus go and pushed him to the floor. Regulus got up and went for Decimus, but he was grabbed and forestalled by two burly soldiers, who pinned his arms up behind his back.

"Let him go. All of you, leave the room and conduct a thorough search of the port," ordered Decimus.

When all the soldiers and rowers had left the room, Decimus spoke to Regulus in a quiet voice.

"Listen, Sabina is a slave, and you are a Roman citizen. She will end the relationship and you will be left heartbroken."

"How do you know?"

"Because that's what happened to me fifteen years ago."

"That's your life, not mine."

"No. Sabina will do it to protect your reputation as a Roman and your position as the Belisama River Pilot."

"I will buy her and set her free by manumission."

"And that raises another problem. Festus is her owner, and he will soon be declared an enemy of the state. All his slaves will be condemned along with him.

You would have to buy her from Festus. Do you honestly think he will agree to a sale?"

Regulus began to calm down.

"I have to try, even if it does mean risking my life."

"You need to think things through. Festus is a first-rate trained swordsman, you are not. What's your plan?"

"I don't know yet."

"Well, you'd better come up with something before you start rushing in with some half-baked idea of taking on a man with an army of rebellious barbarians and treacherous Romans behind him. Now go and prepare the boat for departure on the turn of the tide."

As he turned to leave the room, the older slave girl approached Regulus.

"We saw you coming in the boat, and we have prepared food for all the men."

"You see Decimus, these slaves are obedient and loyal to their posts."

"Very well, we will eat when they have finished preparing things and we have secured Portus Piscium."

Regulus walked down to the boat to begin preparing for sailing on the next tide. As he boarded, he noticed a putrid smell that made him feel sick. The low tide had drained away and revealed the top half of what remained of Stultus sticking out of the slime at the bottom of the creek. Eels slithered around his ribcage, crabs crawled on him, stripping what flesh remained on his bones. Rags of clothing hung from his right arm, which was stuck up in the air at a sixty-degree angle with a skeletal hand that seemed to reach out from some dreadful lower level of the underworld, grasping upward in a vain attempt to pull the living down into a pit of eternal purgatory.

"Best place for you," he said to the rotten remains.

It was then that he noticed Decimus walking along the jetty.

"I must talk with you Regulus."

"Very well, what is it?"

"It's about what happened fifteen years ago."

"Go on," said Regulus.

"Well, you see, the woman who finished things was…" he paused, "it was Seren, your mother."

Chapter Nine
The Last Man Standing

The first light of dawn at Bremetenn had arrived to reveal a village covered in sodden black soot from the smouldering funeral pyres, with acrid smoke still pouring from the dying embers like sinister spirits hanging between the world of the living and the afterlife. Some villagers and soldiers were out on the road, sweeping, cleaning, and repairing, doing what they could to bring some vestiges of normality to life after the carnage and chaos of the day before. Everyone was wondering when Festus and his Brigante army would attack next. Some jollied each other along with speculation that the Legio XX would arrive soon and drive Festus all the way up to the Stanegate Road at the point of a sword.

Sextus and his centurions were organising the soldiers and slaves on the grim task of gathering the ash and charcoal to be thrown in the river, the remains of dead warriors turning the crystal-clear water into a black sludge that moved slowly downstream. All were united in cursing Festus and the Brigantes for what they had done to their way of life, and they all shared the conviction that they would fight to the death before they would let Festus rule any land north of the Belisama. The village Brigantes were Romanised and had no intention of returning to the old tribal ways, which they now considered to be barbaric.

In Lyra's apartment, Seren was preparing to leave and return home, thanking Lyra for her friendship and support in times of trouble and insisting on no charge for Sabina's tunic, which despite all the disruption, she was adamant would be ready soon once she had cleaned her apartment and seen to any damage. Sabina was still inconsolable about her perceived failure to stop open warfare in Britannia, but Lyra and Seren would have none of it, insisting that she was not responsible for Festus's duplicity and the Brigantes' enthusiasm for spilling Roman blood.

Three miles to the north of Bremetenn, Festus and his remaining Brigante chiefs had received news that six centuries of the Legio XX were fording the river at Arma Officinas, and they were deciding what tactic to deploy next. It seemed like the best course of action was a tactical retreat to the Trough Valley, where they could fight the Romans on their own terms. Festus ordered scouts to ride north and bring reinforcements from the Luna River valley and the Lonsdale tribe. He had also received word that a three thousand strong force of Brigante warriors was on its way from the east side of the Pennine Hills and would arrive in the Trough Valley in two days' time. All Festus's warriors were disappointed after the humiliating defeat at Bremetenn, but they consoled themselves with the idea that this was just the start of a war to drive the Romans south of the Belisama and reclaim their ancestral lands.

The Brigantes were convinced that they could force the Emperor Hadrian and the Senate in Rome to the negotiating table, and that the emperor wanted peace throughout the Empire with defined borders and an end to centuries of expansion via military campaigns. After all, the emperor had settled things in Dacia by making concessions of land to the Dacians so if the Dacians could do it, so could the Brigantes and the other tribes of northern Britannia. In the meantime, the Brigantes vowed to give the legions hell and be more trouble than they were worth.

Lyra and Sabina followed Seren back to her apartment to do what they could to help. They found the village blacksmith and one of the carpenters repairing the front door and boarding up the smashed window. Inside, the place had been turned upside down by Brigantes who had sort to escape the lethal crush in the road, but apart from two horse bridles, which Seren had been repairing, nothing had been stolen including the chest bequeathed to her by Gabo, although there were signs that someone had tried to force the lock.

The three women began tidying and cleaning the apartment, and, as Seren lit a fire, the place started to look like a well-kept home once more. Lyra went to see if she could buy some food for Seren, despite there being no market stalls. But at least the baker had fired up his ovens and Lyra, ever the well-paying customer, managed to persuade him to sell her two loaves and a meat pie from his first batch. She returned to Seren's apartment to find the front door fixed and fire crackling in the hearth, spreading its cheerful light and warmth into the room. The warmth and food were more than welcome on such a cold rain-sodden morning and they even managed to laugh a little as conversation began to flow.

As Lyra and Sabina were about to leave and return home, they heard the faint sound of a drum in the distance, beating out a steady rhythm. Sabina had no doubt about the origin of the drum. It was beating out the marching tempo of the Legio XX on the move. They went outside and stood looking up the road towards the brow of the hill north of Bremetenn, waiting for the first soldiers to appear as the drumbeat got louder and the sound of hob nails on gravel became audible. It was not long before the standards of the legion poked up into view above the brow of the hill soon followed by row after row of shining steel, which advanced down the hill. The villagers came out of their homes, lining the road on either side, cheering, clapping, and waving with enthusiasm. Sextus and his centurions stood at the entrance to the fort, ready to greet the legion with all due formalities.

Lyra turned to Sabina:

"You must have seen the Legio XX marching during your years growing up at Deva."

"I did, many times as they practised marching and manoeuvring."

"Does this bring back any memories?"

"Not really."

Lyra bit her lip, not wanting to agitate Sabina.

The Primus Pilus marched past them leading the first century, a leopard skin headdress covering most of his head and face, bearing the golden eagle of the legion. Bremetenn was soon filled with line after line of steel-clad muscle, blood red cloaks, men panting and steaming with sweat after their relentless twenty-four hour forced march. The Primus Pilus and the first century reached Sextus and his centurions and there was a loud call to halt, which was echoed back through the lines as the marching stopped and the soldiers snapped to attention. The villagers stopped cheering and silence fell over Bremetenn. Most, if not all, of the villagers were awestruck by the sight of the legion, especially one so renowned for their fighting prowess and courage. Like most people across the Empire, they had never seen the military machine that made Rome such a super-power.

Sabina began to look at the soldiers' faces in front of her, wondering if she could recognise someone from her days at Deva. Suddenly, a soldier looked straight at her.

"Rufina, is that you?"

Sabina looked at him open-mouthed.

"Rufina, your master has been looking for you."

Sabina shot a question back, "Where is he?"

"At the back, first wagon of auxiliaries."

The centurion in charge of the century whirled round.

"Silence in the ranks!"

The soldier bolted to attention and stared ahead, expressionless.

Sabina set off sprinting up the road with Lyra following as fast as she could as she began to put the pieces together in her head and concluded what she had suspected all along: that Sabina had been stolen from her lawful master and trafficked to Festus.

Sabina continued to sprint with every ounce of energy she could muster until she saw an old, white-haired man sat on a wagon at the back of the assembled soldiers.

She shouted at the top of her voice.

"Master, master, it's me, Rufina."

His eyes were not as sharp as they once were, and Sabina, now six years older and no longer the girl of seven when he had last seen her at Deva. But he began to recognise those distinctive bright green eyes and the wild mop of bright red hair.

"Rufina is that you?" he said, beside himself with surprise.

Sabina leaped onto the wagon and threw her arms around his neck.

"Master, Evander, how I have missed you."

"Where have you been, I thought you had run away."

"No, men took me away. They said they had a scroll that proved you had sold me – three men, one called Stultus, said Festus Crassus, a Prefect of Portus Piscium was my new master."

"I did not sell you. You are documented as a missing slave from Deva. Festus is a liar, a thief, and a traitor to Rome."

"I am so happy to see you again."

"How did you end up here in Bremetenn?"

"I escaped and came here to warn the Romans of Festus's plans. Prefect Sextus has made me his prisoner under the charge of Lyra, his freedwoman. I have been accused of being a runaway slave and dishonouring Festus, my master."

"Why are you now called Sabina?"

"Festus changed my name."

Lyra finally caught up with Sabina.

"Sabina, who is this?"

"This is Evander, my master from Deva."

"Greetings Evander."

"Greetings Lyra."

Evander sat in thought for a moment before speaking.

"Sabina, you must stay with Lyra for now. I can show Sextus that you are indeed my property and we can make good the injustices that have been inflicted upon you."

Lyra was in agreement.

"Yes, I shall speak to Sextus as soon as I can and explain things."

Sabina looked downcast.

"Where shall I find you master?"

"I shall be on the other side of the river with the legion, helping in the kitchens. Now go, I must follow the legion's standards with the rest of the auxiliaries."

Sabina gave him another hug before dismounting and waving him on his way down the road, through the fort, and across the Belisama.

"You've remembered what happened," said Lyra.

"I have. I'd blocked everything out to survive Festus's cruelties, but as soon as I heard that soldier call my old name, it all came back to me like a flood."

"Let's go to my apartment. We must plan our next moves most carefully. The quicksand of Roman laws governing slaves and ownership are treacherous – one false move can prove fatal."

"I trust you Lyra and I will be guided by your advice."

"I will request an audience with Sextus on the way home."

Sextus had finished formal greetings with the Primus Pilus of the Legio XX and returned to his quarters with his centurions. He had received written orders from the Legate at Deva, the supreme commander of the legion and he relayed the orders to his centurions, emphasising that the Austurian Cavalry of Bremetenn was to give full support in attack and defence to the Legio XX.

He had just finished the meeting when there was a knock on the door. Lack of sleep coupled with a wound and the unrelenting stress of recent days had made him short-tempered.

"Yes, what is it?" he snapped.

"Perfect Sextus, Lyra has requested an audience with you."

"Not now!" he rapped sharply, "I will send word when plans with the legion have been completed."

The guard saluted, left, and went back to Lyra who was waiting by the fort north gate.

"I'm sorry Lyra, but he's busy with orders from the Legate. He'll send for you when he has chance."

"Ahh, thank you, I shall wait for word."

And with that Lyra and Sabina went back to Lyra's apartment, dodging soldiers along the way, who were running around preparing things for a state of war with Festus and the Brigantes.

Once back at the apartment, Lyra began to explain her plans to Sabina, and the best way to get her reinstated with her lawful master. There would have to be a hearing before a magistrate to ensure that everything was conducted according to Roman law. The last thing Sabina needed was to find herself being prosecuted for escape and dishonouring her supposed master, Festus Crassus. Far better to seize the initiative and have a hearing as a matter of equity and rightful ownership. Providing Evander would agree to such a hearing and be willing to present testimony and written proof of ownership, the matter was likely to be settled without any complications.

Sabina, not so informed about legal matters, was less than relaxed about going before a magistrate as they had all power to order dreadful sentences upon slaves. If things went wrong, the consequences could be at best being returned to Festus or, at worst, execution.

"What if my master does not have the scroll of ownership?" asked Sabina, fidgeting in her chair.

"We must go to him and find out," said Lyra in her usual calm manner, "and if he does not have it, we must get it from Deva."

"Hmm, that will not be easy, given the state of things at the moment."

"Ahh, let us take things one step at a time," said Lyra with quiet authority, noting that Dido had settled in Sabina's lap.

"You're sure about this?"

"Yes. Far better to be pro-active rather than leave things to chance. Prosecutions are ugly affairs, especially for slaves who have none of the rights afforded to citizens."

Sabina went quiet.

Lyra went on.

"We will give your master time to settle in with the legion before we go and find him. Also, I must wait for word from Sextus."

And then Lyra went quiet, deep in thought about the matter at hand, the silence between them punctuated from time to time by the clatter of soldiers outside. A loud knock on the door startled them and Lyra went to answer. A guard stood waiting.

"Lyra, Prefect Sextus will see you now."

Lyra turned to Sabina.

"Wait here until I return and then we shall seek out Evander."

She followed the guard to find Sextus in his quarters looking grey and haggard, his tunic blood stained on his left side. Lyra could not help but comment.

"Sextus, with all respect to your station, you do not look well."

"I do not feel well," he said, holding his left side with his right hand, "now what's this about?"

"Two things."

"Go on."

"First, now that the Legio XX are here, can we negotiate a peaceful settlement as we discussed earlier?"

"No. I have orders from the Legate at Deva that this rebellion and Festus's treachery are to be crushed by military action. The Legio XX are going to campaign from the Belisama to the Stanegate Road where the Emperor Hadrian plans to set a permanent border to keep the Caledonian tribes in check. The Legio Augusta II are marching towards Bremetenn from their base in Caerleon as we speak and cavalry from Mamucium will be arriving soon to support the cavalry here at Bremetenn. The rebel barbarians and Festus face annihilation. Unconditional surrender is their only hope."

Lyra pursed her lips.

"Then it's all-out war."

"Yes. Governor Falco will have peace before the emperor visits Britannia this summer. He wants to teach the tribes a lesson they will never forget – no more peaceful negotiations."

"I see."

"What was your second item?"

"Ahh, yes, Sabina's rightful master is here with the Legio XX. I wish to present her case to the magistrate as a matter of equity and rightful ownership. It appears she was a victim of slave theft at Deva and trafficked to Portus Piscium."

"I trust you can substantiate the claim with evidence?"

"To the best of my knowledge, yes."

"I see. Very well, if you write the required document, I will sign and seal it, and you can file it with the magistrate."

"Good, I'll explain things in more detail when you are well."

"And when I have more time," he said, shifting in his chair and wincing at the pain from his wound.

"Can I see that wound?" asked Lyra in her most persuasive tone of voice.

Sextus stood and lifted the side of his tunic to reveal a leaking gash, dark red with flecks of lighter red spreading out from the wound.

"By all the gods, you must see a surgeon or the fever will come and take you."

"I do not have time!"

"You will have far less time if you don't go to the infirmary," she responded drily.

Sextus steadied himself on his desk, almost fainting as he did so.

"Come on Sextus," she said softly, "let me take you to the infirmary, I do not want to lose you."

"Have the surgeon come to me."

Lyra went to ask the guard outside to send word to the infirmary. Then she poured some water for Sextus and helped him back in his chair. The surgeon was soon by Sextus's side, inspecting the wound. It did not take him long to conclude that infection was starting to set in and needed prompt attention.

"Lyra, help me take him to the infirmary."

Sextus protested, muttering about not having time to leave his post.

The surgeon was emphatic.

"Prefect Sextus, if you do not get some rest and treatment, you will be dead before two more suns have risen. With treatment, at least you have some chance of recovery."

"Very well, I will come with you, but I can't stay long."

"That may well be the case if treatment does not work."

The surgeon and Lyra helped Sextus to the infirmary and laid him down on one of the beds. Another surgeon, who had arrived at Bremetenn with the Legio XX came over with some opium for the pain and acid vinegar to clean the wound. The surgeons cleaned the wound and placed maggots on the infected area. Lyra said a prayer to Asclepius, the Roman god of healing and medicine, and whispered words of comfort to Sextus as the opium took effect and he fell into a deep, dreamless sleep. She looked at the maggots crawling on the wound with disgust. The surgeon noticed.

"They will clean it by feeding on the infected area. He needs rest now. If the gods are on his side, and the fever breaks, he might pull through."

Lyra nodded and left the infirmary, mindful of the legal document she had been instructed to write, remembering the teachings of her Greek tutor, and the endless lessons on Roman law and politics that she never imagined she would need. All that interminable droning, with death seeming to be the penalty for every transgression plus the endless rules of procedure in the

Senate and the courts. It was enough to drive her to drink so she drank. Still, if it helped Sabina that was, at least, one good thing.

As she was thinking, she walked to her apartment to get Sabina so they could seek out Evander and the all-important scroll of ownership. The two of them walked to the bridge, the sun low in sky as the day rolled into late afternoon, campfires burning between rows of tents to house the four hundred and eighty soldiers and the auxiliaries. At the bridge, they were stopped by guards, asking by what authority they were trying to visit a Legio XX camp.

"We are here on business for Prefect Sextus of Bremetennacum," said Lyra in her best formal Latin."

"Wait here, I will ask our Primus Pilus for permission to let you through," said the guard and he disappeared into the camp. He returned with the Primus Pilus, who addressed Lyra with dry formality.

"Madam, please state your business in the camp of the Legio XX."

"I am charged with writing a legal document on behalf of Prefect Sextus. One of your auxiliaries, known as Evander, is in possession of vital evidence, which must be presented to the magistrate."

"In the matter of what?"

"In the matter of disputed slave ownership."

"Very well, but there are many Evanders in the camp."

"Ahh, I see. This one is old and he was on the first auxiliary wagon behind the soldiers."

"That would be Evander, the 'Last Man Standing'. I will escort you to him. A legion camp is no place for a lady."

They followed the Primus Pilus towards a kitchen area, but at that point, Lyra would have followed him into the lower regions of Hades. She was thunderstruck, giddy, and had to use all her willpower to stay collected and in control on this vital mission, forcing back the urge to giggle, her stomach alive with butterflies. Never had she felt such a magnetic attraction towards a man. Sabina followed three steps behind, head bowed, aware of soldiers in the camp staring at her and Lyra, making her feel uncomfortable and nervous.

The kitchen area was a buzzing hive of frenetic activity. Whole pigs roasted on spits above fires, wheat was being ground to flour for fresh bread, amphora of olives and olive oil laid out ready, all to feed the soldiers and auxiliaries after their gruelling march from Deva. Soldiers were lining up, all of them ravenous with hunger. Evander doddered about helping where he could, but it was clear that he had seen better days.

The Primus Pilus called to Evander.

"Evander, there is a lady here to see you on business for Prefect Sextus."

Evander turned and saw Sabina.

"Rufina, you are here," he said, delighted to see her again, "and Lyra, greetings, how may I be of service?"

It was all Lyra could do to stop staring at the Primus Pilus, but she collected herself and clung to the matter at hand.

"I need the scroll of ownership for Sabina in order to write a legal appeal to the magistrate."

"Why are you doing that?"

"Because we must get equitable relief that you are Sabina's rightful owner. Officially, Sabina is an escaped slave, a prisoner of Prefect Sextus under my charge.

If Festus were to prosecute a claim, Sabina could be in jeopardy for her life."

"Festus will not live that long. He and his ragbag army of barbarians are going to be crushed. They are facing the Legio XX and the Legio Augusta II."

"I understand, but if he surrenders, he will be sentenced to death and his slaves along with him. If we pre-empt things now, so much the better."

Evander stood in thought for a moment.

"I see, very well, wait here please."

And with that he trudged off towards the auxiliary tents.

It was then that Lyra noticed the Primus Pilus looking at her. She looked straight back as he spoke.

"Madam, I will wait here with you until it is time to escort you back to the bridge."

Lyra spoke with formality, but her tone was as soft as a feather bed.

"I thank you for your kindness and good manners sir."

Sabina glanced up at the two of them, and for the first time in her life she felt the sharp pang of jealousy. She shivered at being left out in the cold, forced apart from the warmth of attraction between Lyra and the Primus Pilus. She wanted to tell Lyra to stop, to tell this man to leave her alone, strange emotions of anger, hurt, and resentment welling up inside her mixing with a feeling of nausea deep in the pit of her stomach. She kept her head bowed as her feelings seethed unseen.

Evander returned holding a small scroll and handed it to Lyra.

"Here and let me know if you need me to testify in support of its authenticity."

"I will."

"I meant to ask, her given name is Rufina, why do you call her Sabina?"

"Because Festus changed her name to make her appear more high-born and increase the price when it came time to sell her."

"Festus is such a thief and dishonourable liar."

"On that we can agree."

Lyra turned to the Primus Pilus.

"May I ask you for your name sir?"

"My name is Cyrus. May I ask you for your name?"

"Lyra, and this slave under my charge is Sabina."

"I am pleased to make your acquaintance," he said, standing rock solid to attention.

"You have been the perfect gentleman. I would like to ask Prefect Sextus to invite you to the next dinner party for legionary leaders, that is, if it pleases you."

"That would be an honour, but I am under orders to pursue the barbarians and engage them in battle when the legions are assembled."

"Of course, but perhaps when the legions have restored the Peace of Rome?"

"Certainly. Allow me to escort you back to the bridge."

At the bridge, as they bid their farewells, Lyra's curiosity got the better of her.

"Forgive me for asking, but why is Evander referred to as the last man standing?"

"Because he is the last surviving member of the Legio XX that fought against Boudicca in the great final battle."

"But that was sixty-one years ago!"

"Yes, he was twenty-one at the time. He enlisted when he was fourteen, and although he retired decades ago, he is still devoted to his brothers in the twentieth. Where we go, he goes."

"I see, farewell and may the gods go with you."

"And also with you."

As Lyra and Sabina crossed the bridge, Sabina could not hold back.

"You seem quite taken with Cyrus."

"Ahh, he is the most gorgeous man I have ever set eyes on."

They entered the apartment and Sabina sat down with a bump, consumed with jealousy. Dido came to sit in her lap, but she brushed her aside with an impatient push.

Lyra sat down next to her.

"Don't be like that – after all, you love Regulus."

"I know, it, well, it does not make any sense."

"Ahh," said Lyra with a smile, "for all my education, I find making sense of life and love quite impossible."

"It's not fair!" said Sabina with outraged indignation, "why do I have these feeling for you and Regulus?"

Lyra was most matter of fact in her response.

"Well, sooner or later you will have to make your mind up, but I did warn you that what happened between us was just sex."

Sabina was furious.

"Don't trivialise things, you make me feel small and used."

"How dare you lecture me. We both enjoyed ourselves and that's that. I'm trying to save your life and all you can do is rant at me with childish possessiveness. You're a grown woman so act like one."

Tears began to run down Sabina's face. She stormed out of the apartment, slammed the door behind her, and went to the edge of the riverbank. She shivered in the cold evening air, staring at the rows of tents and campfires on the opposite bank, trying to make sense of something that did not make sense. She remembered how she had hidden her emotions when she was a slave at Portus Piscium, how she stayed one step ahead of the constant deprivation and brutality along with the burning injustices of captivity and forced labour. It worked for her then, so why not now? But the more she tried, the tighter the icy grip of jealousy became.

She wanted to run. Run towards the moon with the tide on her heels. Run with wind in her hair. Run towards freedom outwitting those who stood in her way. Run away from the feelings that overwhelmed her and made her a prisoner. Run like she had done out on the marshes of the Belisama estuary.

But there was nowhere to run. She had to face things and somehow overcome, collect herself and move forward here, in Bremetenn. She was a prisoner of Rome, confined to a prison without locks, walls, and bars. She turned and walked back to Lyra's apartment, wiping her eyes as she went. She entered the apartment sheepishly, ready to apologise for her outburst. Lyra sat, quill in hand, writing by the light of oil lamps, each letter and punctuation mark crafted with meticulous care to form the legal appeal to the magistrate. Sabina did not dare interrupt.

Lyra raised her head.

"It's all right, but I must finish this soon. Sextus may die in the infirmary if his wound does not heal, which would render this document useless without his signature and seal.

"I'm sorry," said Sabina.

"So am I, I never meant to hurt you."

Sabina nodded and Lyra went back to the task at hand, recognising the dark pitiless shadow of punishment that awaited Sabina if she failed.

Chapter Ten
Lockbox

Winter had forgotten that spring had arrived. Gale force winds blew with howling gusts, and bone-chilling rain marched across the marshes of the Belisama estuary in black veils, the tide battling against the wind, throwing up steep waves with white crests, foaming off the water. Decimus stood on the jetty, facing off against Regulus as the tide started to float the *Belisama Cygnus*.

"Explain what?" said Regulus.

"That I was a Primus Pilus and your mother was still a slave. You know Roman law forbids marriage between people of those statuses. Your mother saw no future for us, so she ended our love affair."

"Are you saying you are my father?"

"I am."

Regulus jumped off the boat and landed his fist in Decimus's face. He might as well have hit a stone wall. He tried to hit him again, but Decimus caught his hand and twisted his wrist. Regulus was on the floor with his arm locked, stunned by the speed and strength of Decimus's defence.

"Stop this, I don't want to hurt you."

Regulus looked up at him. In each other's eyes, they saw each other: unyielding, fearless, and stubborn.

Regulus snarled at him.

"So you left my mother in slavery, pregnant, and destitute."

"If you would calm down and let me, explain. It was not like that."

"Really, what was it like?" fumed Regulus.

"Your mother and Gabo were firm friends, as were Gabo and me. We all agreed that Gabo would be a father figure in your life and I would see to it you were born a free Roman citizen. I made sure that the old couple would free Seren before you were born, but they both died within days of each other, and Seren was freed according to their will. Everything was done in secret to benefit you and your mother, including me giving your mother money for food and rent in times of hardship."

Decimus relaxed his grip and Regulus stood up, still raging with anger and frustration, trying to make sense of what he was being told. Was Decimus trying to cover for himself? But then he remembered the unexplained brief visits to his home, Decimus being around with Gabo when they went hunting deer, and fishing for the great salmon in the river in the spring and autumn. It was Decimus that taught him how to ride a horse and wield a sword.

"Why wait until now to tell me this big secret?"

"We were going to tell you when you became a man. Then Gabo was murdered and what with all this cack storm that Festus has caused..."

"Well thank you for that, but now I feel like my life has been one big lie."

Decimus raised his voice.

"No, look at yourself. You are strong and healthy, a respected River Pilot with citizen status and a good income. You have a caring mother and those who look out for your best interests."

Regulus was about to reply when the older of the two slave girls came onto the jetty, hands clasped in front of her and head bowed. She addressed the two of them formally.

"Primus Pilus, Fluvius Gabanator, I have something to show you."

"What is it?" snapped Regulus, impatient to ask Decimus more questions.

The slave girl fell to her knees.

"Forgive me Fluvius Gabanator. I wanted to show you where Prefect Festus Crassus has hidden his fortune."

Regulus and Decimus looked at each other in disbelief.

"Please, rise and show us," said Regulus.

She led them to the warehouse and into Festus's bedroom. Then, she pointed to a wooden panel behind the bedhead.

"Lift the panel and there's a lockbox in the wall space," she said, and bowed her head.

They lifted the panel and pulled the one-foot square lockbox out of the wall space. It was heavy and sturdy, with two iron bands, all secured with a padlock and clasp. Decimus left the room and returned with a hammer and chisel. He hammered away at the padlock and clasp until they snapped. They raised the lid and what they saw took their breath away. It was full of gold and silver coins.

"Well," said Regulus, "now I know how I can buy Sabina's freedom."

"We must take this to Bremetenn and present it to Sextus. Stop talking nonsense about squandering it on a slave."

"We must sail soon, or we will miss the tide," replied Regulus, thinking about more personalised arrangements for the money.

Decimus ordered the other soldiers to stay at Portus Piscium, assuring them that reinforcements would be sent as soon as he arrived at Bremetenn. Regulus and Dadas loaded the lockbox onto the boat and prepared to sail. The tide had filled the creek and the boat was afloat. Decimus jumped aboard and Regulus ordered full sail. The boat forged ahead in the squally gale, past the Arma Officinas where they could see another cohort of the Legio XX waiting to ford the river at low tide and march onwards to Bremetenn. On they went in the dim late afternoon light, the rowers pulling hard so would stand a chance of arriving at Bremetenn before nightfall.

The urgency of the voyage gave no time for conversation between Regulus and Decimus, but the rowers, especially Dadas, could sense an atmosphere that was colder than the weather. Decimus stood at the front of the boat on the lookout for rogue Brigantes and Regulus manning the steering oar, alert for shallow water now the tides were not as high. One false move could ground the boat leaving them exposed and vulnerable to an attack.

Regulus knew that a few of the silver coins would be more than enough to buy Sabina's freedom. He began to scheme elaborate scenarios to get his hands on some of the coins, oblivious, of course, to Lyra's plan, which was unfolding at the same time. In any case, how was he going to buy her from a treacherous Roman who was heading up an army of barbarians against Rome? Still, he thought, money talks and things could always be arranged for the right price. It was yet to dawn on him that he would be attempting to buy Sabina from Festus with his own ill-gotten money.

Late afternoon passed and segued into the twilight gloom of evening. They had sailed beyond the tidal reaches of the river, and the rowers had to pull harder against the downstream flow, which was swollen and in full spate from the persistent and heavy rainfall. The only thing that kept them moving was the wind blowing hard from behind them, filling the sail and driving them forward. Decimus abandoned his post at the front and manned the sail, Regulus shouting instructions as he steered the boat, keeping to the deeper sections, thankful that they were not carrying cargo or soldiers.

As darkness began to fall, an ersatz sunrise to the east of them cast a yellow glow in the distance. At first, Regulus was puzzled until he realised it was the collective light from numerous campfires and torches burning in the darkness. He steered with caution, following the outline of the riverbanks, remembering where the deeper sections of the river lay, especially on the bends. The fort came into view and soon they were surrounded by soldiers who were bathing in the river, laughing, and splashing each other, washing the dirt, and sweat off themselves after their long march from Deva. The village was alive with market stalls, eager to profit from the sudden influx of men with money to spend. Some of the women had dressed their best and walked about plying their own style of welcome and trade. The queue for the bath house was endless.

Regulus brought the boat alongside the loading dock and some of the soldiers came down from the fort to give them a warm welcome, pleased to see them back safe, knowing what a hazardous mission they had undertaken. Everyone had a story to tell: the attack on the fort, the battles at Arma Officinas, Decimus at the Hill Fort, the timely arrival of the Legio XX, and how Festus and barbarian horde were going to rue the day they picked a fight with Rome.

Seren had heard the cheering from her apartment and she made her way down to the river. She gasped with relief when she saw her son unharmed. She flung her arms around him and as she did so, Decimus caught her eye. He did not speak audibly, but mouthed, "he knows". She got the message, but this was no time for family discussions.

"It is wonderful to see you home; I have been so worried."

"You worry too much. It seems the Brigantes are finding me a hard man to kill."

Seren looked her son straight in the eye.

"You must go and see Sabina. She's at Lyra's apartment and she has much to tell you."

"Well, whatever it is, I'll find it hard to be surprised. Today has been full of surprises."

"Then go and see her."

"I will do, but first I must go with Decimus and report to Sextus."

"Do what you must. I will prepare supper and have it ready when you come home."

"I thank you mother. It feels good to be home and see you well."

Decimus and Regulus humped the hefty lockbox up to Sextus's chamber, only to find him absent. One of the guards told them that he was in a bad way at the infirmary. They went to visit to see if could give them instructions as to where to store the lockbox. They found him lying on one of the beds, sound asleep with maggots shuffling about on his exposed wound. He looked ghastly and at death's door. One of the infirmary slaves came over.

"Primus Pilus, Fluvius Gabanator, our Prefect is not well. The surgeon has serious doubts about whether he will live to see sunrise and I am under strict instructions to make sure he is not disturbed. He needs sleep and time to heal."

"Very well but tell him I came to report when he wakes," said Decimus.

"As instructed," said the slave as he bowed and went to attend to another patient.

"Now what?" asked Regulus.

"We shall secure the lockbox in one of the prison cells and wait for further instructions."

"Very well, but then I must go and see Sabina."

Decimus huffed and puffed.

"You have not heard a word I have said."

They went to the prison cells, and Decimus told the jailor a fictitious story about the box containing vital evidence for a forthcoming trial, and that they would be back later with the suspect. The jailor, bored and disinterested as usual on his lonely night vigil, shrugged, and locked the cell door.

Regulus turned away and headed for Lyra's apartment. Elaborate schemes about how to get his hands on some of the coins still rattled around in his head. While he knew that theft was a crime, he regarded stealing from Festus more like a public service, rebalancing the scales of justice against a sadistic avaricious traitor. He was so wrapped up in his thoughts that he was surprised to find himself at Lyra's door. He knocked, Sabina answered, and she screamed with joy as she jumped on him, arms around his neck and legs around his waist. The long deep kiss that followed silenced them both. Lyra watched and smiled.

Sabina explained what had happened with Evander, and Lyra's plan to petition the magistrate to make sure she was legally protected by her rightful owner. Regulus regaled his tales about the battles at Arma Officinas, and Festus's gold and silver coins hidden away in the lockbox behind a concealed panel. The moment he mentioned the gold and silver coins, Lyra began to question him.

"Were is the lockbox now?"

"Locked in one of the prison cells."

"Who else knows about this?"

"Decimus, one of the slave girls at Portus Piscium, and now you and Sabina."

"Are you sure there is no one else?"

"Dadas and the prison jailor know about the box, but they have no idea what's in it."

"Ah, very good."

"Why do you ask?"

"It's for your own safety. And now I must get this document signed and sealed by Sextus."

"I've just seen him at the infirmary. He's unconscious and terribly ill."

"All the more reason to make haste," said Lyra as she slipped into her long black cloak and glided out of the apartment."

For the first time since their mission to get Decimus into the Hill Fort, Regulus and Sabina were alone together. They sat facing each other, holding hands, talking, and kissing."

"Sabina, I adore you and I want to marry you."

"Yes, I will happily marry you, but first we must go along with Lyra's plan and make certain that Festus has no claim of ownership over me."

"By Juno, I hate that man so much."

"So do I...all those years of abuse and cruelty under Festus and Stultus. Anyway, the Legio XX will take care of Festus."

"Of that I have no doubt. Anyway, come and have supper with my mother."

"I have another idea."

She led him to the spare bedroom.

"What if Lyra returns?"

She could not help a wry smile, thinking about how Lyra would put it down to "just sex".

"Lyra is liable to be a while."

She gave Regulus a deep long kiss and at that point he was beyond caring if the Vestal Virgins came trooping through let alone the ever-promiscuous Lyra. They made love, passionately and hurried at first with words of adoration. Then, they laid next to each, caressing and exploring each other, slow at first until they were ready to climax again, taking the time to express themselves through their bodies until they were wrapped in a haze of contended bliss.

"You should go home now, Lyra will return soon and you should not disappoint your mother," whispered Sabina.

"You should come with me."

"I would love to, but I can't. I'm still under Lyra's charge so I must look after the apartment and the cat until she returns and gives me permission."

Regulus stood and dressed himself.

"Hurry back my love."

"I will, I promise."

He walked from the apartment and up the road towards home feeling the happiest he had ever been in his life. At last he saw a way of marrying Sabina, the love of his life, and being with her forever. Of course, he would have to buy her from Evander, but he felt optimistic, and he was sure something could be worked out. Ultimately, he thought, if he could persuade Decimus to keep the gold and silver coins, money would be the ultimate tool of persuasion.

His thoughts were interrupted by fist fights, which had spilled out of the tavern and onto the road; ridiculous drunken brawls accompanied by a great deal of ranting and shouting about gambling disputes and who was going home with which woman. He detoured around them on the opposite side of the road, knowing all too well how easy it was to become embroiled in fights with drunken soldiers. Fighting and brutality was their stock in trade and one wrong look in their direction was enough to spark violence.

He entered his mother's apartment to find Decimus sitting at the table with her. She rose to welcome her son home.

"What's he doing here?" he asked, barely able to hold back his indignation.

Seren embraced her son and spoke in a quiet reassuring voice.

"Don't be so impatient. We want to talk to you and explain a few things - make sure you get the whole story. Come, sit, you must ravenous."

"Yes, I am hungry, but I'm not sure I want to hear what you have to say."

He sat down as Seren served the three of them a venison stew with bread left over from Lyra's visit. Regulus was glad and grateful for the hot food and the warmth of home on such a cold damp night. But he was wary and uncomfortable with Decimus sat at the table. Still, he thought, now was as good a time as any to broach his plan to take possession of the lockbox.

"Decimus, why don't we keep the lockbox for ourselves?"

"What?" he thundered, "that's stealing from Emperor Hadrian and the Empire, and that's wrong, quite apart from the fact that it's enough to get us both executed."

"The Empire does not know of its existence. It's blood money and besides, the Empire and Emperor are swimming in gold and wealth."

"It is still theft, it is wrong, and it violates Roman law. You're not thinking straight. Oh, wait, it's that cursed slave woman that's turned your head. Get a grip on yourself."

"Well, to Hades with you," shouted Regulus at the top of his voice, "that money could do so much good: buy you land and horse breeding stock for your retirement, finance the river economy, security for my mother, I could on, and all that investment would create more wealth."

"By all the gods, think!" roared Decimus at the top of his voice, "it's still theft."

"Only if we get caught."

Seren was angry and upset at father and son arguing.

"Get out, both of you. Get the cursed box and hand it over to the Legio XX Primus Pilus or the Legate when he arrives."

"That is what we shall do," said Decimus.

Regulus sat back in his chair burning with frustration.

"What a waste of an opportunity."

Seren was adamant.

"Do it. Don't come back until you've handed every coin over and settled the argument."

The two of them left Seren's apartment and trudged down the road with their tails between their legs. The market stalls were still buzzing and the brawls in and outside the tavern were still in full swing. They arrived at the infirmary to find Sextus propped up on a pillow, a slave encouraging him to sip some hot soup. The slave looked up at Decimus and Regulus, concern written all over his face.

"Please, with all respect, the Prefect needs food and rest."

Sextus waved them to come to come forward.

"Decimus, be advised that I have charged Lyra with the day-to-day administration of Bremetenn until I am well enough to return. The accounts clerk will take care of the finances. I..." and he fell back to sleep as more opium took over his senses, embracing him on a soft cushion of pain relief.

Decimus assumed authority.

"Let's go, get the lockbox, and take it to the Legio XX Primus Pilus."

They went to the prison cell to find the cell door open and no lockbox.

"What the…" said Decimus, only to be interrupted by a scathing Regulus.

"Brilliant, just brilliant. Robbed from under our noses. Now what?"

"The jailor, it must be him, he's got the key."

The jailor was sound asleep, snoring like a hibernating bear, an empty jug in his right hand. Decimus snatched the jug away and sniffed it. Wine. He slapped the jailor hard.

"Wake up stupid!"

"Er, um, what, what's going on?"

Decimus seized the jailor by his lapels and dragged him to his feet."

"The lockbox in cell four. Where is it?"

"Eh? It's still there."

"Don't try that one."

"I swear I don't know what you're talking about. Get off me."

"Get off you? I have not even got started you impudent piece of vermin. Talk, or I'll have you flogged raw."

"I'm telling you, I don't know what you're on about. Must have fallen asleep. A woman came with wine. Said everyone was celebrating the coming of the Legio XX. Said she had been sent to show me a good time. The wine. Cack. Must have passed out."

"Who was she and who sent her?"

Regulus interrupted, "Decimus, smell this jug again. He's been drugged."

Decimus was beside himself with fury and threw the jailor on the bed.

"Idiot! Duped by the oldest trick in the book. Not one word about this to anyone, or I will personally see to your execution."

The jailor nodded and passed out, overwhelmed by the drugs and wine.

Decimus and Regulus went back to Sextus's quarters to find Lyra sat behind the desk, head down, quill in hand, writing with her usual delicate strokes.

"How lovely to see you both," she said.

Decimus was taken aback to see a woman sat in Sextus's chair.

"We are here to report a theft."

"Of what?"

"Festus's lockbox, which we had secured in one of the prison cells."

"Ahh, I see. Well, I am only here to administrate the day-to-day matters of running of Bremetenn until Sextus recovers. The clerk is taking care of money matters."

"As Primus Pilus of the fort cavalry, I intend to conduct a full investigation."

"Yes of course, a full investigation and I shall make a note of your intentions. Now, while you are here, I have a document for you from the Legate of the Legio XX via his couriers. You are to prepare the cavalry to support the legion in the campaign against Festus. You will be joined by the cavalry from Mamucium in the morning. The Legate is to arrive in the morning with the final cohort of the Legio XX. You are to report to him as soon as he arrives for further orders."

Decimus read the orders.

"I must go now and prepare the men."

"Very well. Regulus, you are to commence reviving peaceful trade with the Portus Piscium and the Setantii as soon as the tides are favourable. Also, I have filed to have Sabina's case to be heard by the magistrate tomorrow afternoon if you would like to attend."

"I would. I shall call on you in the morning."
"And now it seems we all have much to do."
Regulus looked Decimus straight in the eye.
"Mars protect you Roman."
"And you."

❀❀❀❀❀❀❀❀

Sextus woke in the small hours of the morning to find the area around his bed illuminated by a strange light. At first, he thought someone had been kind enough to light multiple oil lamps or candles, but that did not quite fit. He noticed that the pain and weariness from his festering wound had gone and there, at the end of the bed, stood his late wife, hand reaching out for him as he sat up and got to his feet. He took her hand, happy to see her once again after almost five years, and the two of them slipped into the afterlife. And so died Sextus: Roman warrior, Prefect, and loyal citizen of the Roman Empire.

Chapter Eleven
Magistrate

The night that Sextus passed, the fort and the village of Bremetenn were alive with frenzied activity. Decimus and his centurions barked orders at the cavalry as they ran around preparing the horses for presentation to the Legate, who was due to arrive soon after dawn. The horses had to washed and brushed, saddles polished until they shone, armour to be polished, swords, arrows, and spears to be sharpened. Decimus was determined that this was to be his last action for the Legio XX and his secondment to the cavalry of Bremetenn. He was not going to have his otherwise exemplary legionary service marred by presenting a scruffy cavalry under his command to the Legate.

Fresh metal and leather shoes for the horses, Hipposandals, were in peak demand with the blacksmith and his assistants drafted in to work through the night. Seren beavered away by candlelight, stitching, and repairing as many leather bridle leather straps as she could, Regulus and the rowers worked on making the *Belisama Cygnus* shine, and Sabina set to making the apartment spotless so it was ready for any entertainment required by the Legio XX officers. Lyra was doing her best to make arrangements for Sextus's funeral while dealing with necessary documents for the day to day running of the fort and the village. It was a night where sleep at Bremetenn was a rare commodity.

First light brought the promise of a perfect spring day as the rising sun revealed a cloudless sky. The cavalry from Mamucium added to the relentless activity in the village until both cavalry units cantered up the road to the northern defence line to wait at the top of the Belisama valley for the Legate to arrive with the final cohort of infantry. Over four thousand legionaries were assembled on the defence line, supported by eight hundred cavalrymen from Bremetenn and Mamucium. Auxiliaries with wagons loaded with food and weapons were still arriving, sheep and cattle were being herded into pens, chicken coups erected, and tents lined the ridge.

Fifteen feet high wooden lookout towers stood like giants every hundred yards along a ditch, which marked the defence line. Catapults and ballista machines were in position with their operators busy stocking up boulders and oil pots ready for deployment at the first order. Breakfast porridge bubbled and steamed in pots hung over a hundred fires and everyone ate on feet when and where they could between carrying out their duties, all the while eyeing the enemy line in the distance, watching to see if there was any sign of an advance. To those on the watchtowers, it was clear that, at least for now, Festus and his army were staying put.

The sun had climbed a little higher in the east over the Pennine Hills when the Legate and his officers came into view from the west. Word flashed around the legion. They formed up with their respective centurions, shields in front of them, holding their spears upright. Decimus formed up the cavalry in a line, some of the horses champing on their bits, pawing the ground, snorting steam into the cold early morning air. Cyrus and his cohort, the fastest and most elite of all the cohorts in the legion, stood ready to be the first to greet the Legate and report.

The Legate arrived with his officers, dismounted from his horse, and began his inspection of the legion. He walked up and down the lines at a slow even pace, looking straight into the eyes of the men, each man knowing that unfailing loyalty, obedience, and dedication to the legion was expected even unto death, or face eternal disgrace on themselves and their family name. The bond of brotherhood and camaraderie in the legions of Rome was unbreakable and perhaps more so in the Legio XX with their record of courage and victories across their campaigns.

Once the inspection was completed, the officers followed the Legate into his large marquee, which served as a command centre. Decimus and the Primus Pilus from Mamucium followed to receive their final orders for the cavalry. For the soldiers outside, it was time to take a rest period and finish the breakfast porridge. If they were going to be ordered into battle today, which looked likely, this would be the last chance to get some rest and eat. The rest period was short lived as alarm bells rang out from the tops of the towers. All the men stood and went to the defence line to see what the alarm signified. There were five men on horseback under a flag of truce, and they stopped a hundred yards from the defence line: four Brigante chiefs and Festus Crassus.

The Legate and four of his officers mounted their horses and went out at a slow walking pace to meet Festus and the Brigantes. Time seemed to stop as the whole Roman army fell silent and stood still, knowing that the outcome of whatever transpired from the meeting would determine future action or inaction. Many of the Romans were spoiling for a fight to finish off rebellions in Britannia for good, viewing the native people of the dark rain-plagued island as backward uncivilized barbarians, only good for slave labour and entertainment in the arena.

The Legate was the first to speak.

"Festus Crassus, what is it that you want?"

"Peace be with you Legate, I seek not bloodshed but only wish to negotiate with you. We seek a border with the Empire from the Belisama to the Abus Fluvius so the tribes can form a confederation."

The Legate was firm and spoke with disdain.

"There will be no negotiations. You, and all the tribes of the north will offer unconditional surrender with immediate effect."

"Let us be reasonable, the tribes want their ancestral lands returned. A new confederation of tribes and the Roman Empire can co-exist in peace with profit for all," said Festus like he was negotiating a business deal.

"You will surrender now. If you do not, a state of war will exist between Rome and your barbarians of the north."

Festus tried again.

"Come come, we both know Emperor Hadrian intends to set up a border along the Stanegate Road. Why not here, barely a hundred miles to the south?"

"No, and that is final. Emperor Hadrian has defined the Britannia border and I have my orders. You are a traitor to the emperor, the leader of a murderous collection of barbarian scum, and you will surrender to Roman authority now."

"Since you will not be reasonable, it seems we have nothing further to talk about."

Festus and the four chiefs turned and rode away. The Legate and his officers turned and began riding back towards the legion. As they rode the Legate turned to his officers.

"You have your orders, prepare to take the field against our enemy. The ram has touched the wall."

"Hail Ceasar!" they replied as one.

Mid-day approached and Sabina was becoming more agitated by the minute. Lyra returned to the apartment with Evander and Regulus ready to attend the magistrate's hearing scheduled for the afternoon. Despite Dido's best efforts to get in the way, Sabina had cleaned and tidied the apartment from top to bottom ready for any formal visits by the Legate and his officers. Word that a great battle was coming had spread around Bremetenn and all the civilians could do was carry on with the chores of everyday life, keeping faith with the Roman army's ability to crush the rebellion as they had done with other rebellions throughout the centuries of Roman rule.

"We should make our way over to the courthouse," said Lyra, assuming authority and responsibility for the hearing.

"Hmm, are you still sure this is the right way to go about things?" asked Sabina.

Lyra was vexed.

"Yes, and stop asking, I've explained why and schooled you in how to respond to possible awkward questions about your escape. We must go now."

The four of them walked over to the courtroom in silence and, once there, took their seats outside waiting to be called before the magistrate. Regulus and Lyra were doing their best to keep Sabina calm, when things took a dramatic turn for the worst. A slave was dragged into the courtroom by two guards. The door was left open, so the four of them craned around the entrance to see and hear what was happening. The hapless slave stood before the magistrate in chains as a charge of murder was read out loud by the court clerk.

The hearing was short. The slave had spilled some wine on his master's clean white toga and the master had taken to beating him with a stick. The slave had begged forgiveness for being so clumsy, but as the beating continued, the slave had pushed his master away. The master had fallen backwards, smashed his head on a tiled floor, and died where he lay. The magistrate reasoned that because the slave liked to fight back, he could do just that in the arena at Deva against professional gladiators and entertain the audience with his fighting prowess. It was a sentence the slave would not survive.

Sabina's hearing was called as the terrified slave was dragged out of the courtroom, shouting about how the whole thing was a dreadful accident and pleading for mercy. One of the guards told the slave to be grateful that he had avoided crucifixion and that it was honourable to die with a sword in hand. The slave did not see things quite the same way. Sabina was shaken by pity for the slave and worried about how things could go the wrong way for her hearing. She entered the courtroom behind Lyra while Regulus and Evander stood at the back, waiting to be called as witnesses.

The magistrate sat on a large purple padded chair, which was mounted on a podium. He was a thin grey-haired man with a sharp hooked nose like an eagle's beak. His piecing blue eyes skewered those who stood beneath him as their lives hung on the scales of Roman justice. Sabina stood before him with her head bowed as Lyra moved to one side and the clerk of the court read out the pleadings for relief. The magistrate listened to the clerk and addressed the court.

"What a strange case," he muttered, "where is the man they call Evander?"

Evander stepped forward.

"I am here magistrate."

"And you claim to be the rightful owner of this slave?"

"I do."

"Clerk, hand me the scroll of ownership."

The magistrate read the scroll and handed it back.

"I see – how can you be sure that the young slave Rufina did not run away and escape from you?"

"Because she was a child of integrity, honour, and always told the truth."

"And you testify with your honour?"

"With all my honour as an auxiliary of Legio XX with over sixty years of service, thirty of those years as a serving legionary and centurion."

The magistrate sat back in his chair.

"Has the slave been tortured according to the law?"

Lyra stepped forward.

"Magistrate, if it pleases you, Prefect Sextus ordered me to conduct the interrogation."

"You, a woman?"

"Yes, I have been his official interrogator for four years."

"Slave, I am concerned that you escaped from Portus Piscium in full knowledge that Festus Crassus was your master."

Sabina shuffled about nervously.

"Hmm, I erm…"

Evander stepped forward.

"Magistrate, with your permission."

"You may speak."

"The slave Rufina, now called Sabina, is my property. Under the law is up to me what I do with my slaves."

"True enough, however as magistrate, it is up to me to see that the law is upheld and justice is best served. And I would remind you that this is my court."

"My apologies magistrate," said Evander as he bowed and stepped back.

"Speak slave!"

"Magistrate, I escaped to come to Bremetenn and warn Rome about Festus's treachery and the plot to ferment a dangerous rebellion. I risked my life to do so, and in doing so, I have shown loyalty and service to the greater good of Rome."

"Do not lecture me about loyalty and service to Rome. You are a slave, and a slave's first duty is to his or her master or mistress".

Sabina's legs turned to jelly, but she knew she had to hold herself together. She took a deep breath and answered as Lyra had instructed.

"Magistrate, I knew Prefect Festus Crassus was not my rightful owner. I always longed to be back at Deva with Evander, who I had been with since birth."

The magistrate looked at her with cold dispassionate eyes, vexed by such a forthright reply from a slave. He took to reading the petition once more, drumming the arm of the chair with his fingers as he read. Sabina stood feeling vulnerable and small, wishing that the ground would open up and swallow her as she died a hundred times inside. Then the magistrate stood and announced that he wished to adjourn the hearing while he studied the petition before making a ruling. Sabina, Lyra, Evander, and Regulus trooped out of the courtroom to wait until the magistrate reconvened the hearing.

They sat in silence, knowing that there was a real possibility that the magistrate could rule against the petition and conclude that Sabina was guilty of escaping from her master and dishonouring his name. There was no doubt that if things did turn out that way, Sabina would be executed, and for the first time, Lyra began to doubt herself. Sabina was wishing she was anywhere but here. Regulus held Sabina's hand trying to comfort the love of his life as she stared ashen faced into space. Time dragged and came to a standstill in the endless wait.

A guard announced that the magistrate was ready to reconvene and ushered them back into the courtroom. The iron manacles hanging from his belt did not bode well.

Once the magistrate was satisfied that the court was assembled, and everything was in order, he announced that the hearing was in session.

"The slave Rufina, also known as Sabina, step forward."

Sabina stepped forward into the middle of the cold tiled floor, ice flowing through her veins, her stomach turning and churning.

"This is indeed an unusual case, but I do find the witness testimony compelling since Evander and Lyra are loyal and honourable subjects of Emperor Hadrian and the Empire. At face value, I find the scroll of ownership to be authentic. As to whether or not this slave escaped or was abducted by slave thieves at Deva, I cannot judge because there is no evidence to support either. I am, however, aware that slave theft and trafficking those slaves for service is rife across the Empire, costing honest citizens thousands of talents. I rule that this slave is the property of Evander, loyal servant of Rome, and honourable member of the Legio XX in which he has served with distinction. Next case."

Sabina stood where she was, numb from head to toe as Lyra moved forward, took her by the arm, and led her from the courtroom. Evander waited for the clerk to finish a written ruling with the magistrate's seal upon it. Regulus was beside himself with relief and joy. At last he saw the way clear to make her his wife as the dark shadow of Festus lifted. He rushed over and put his arms around her, holding her close. Lyra let go of Sabina's arm and stood beaming from ear to ear at the lovers locked together. Evander came out of the courtroom with the sealed ruling and another scroll.

Lyra had another reason to be happy. Not only had she been instrumental in saving Sabina's life, but she had also had sight of Sextus's will in which she had been made a Roman citizen. Never again would she have to endure the horrors of standing on a platform, under the auctioneer's hammer at a slave market. Also, because Sextus had no surviving family members, there was the bonus of inheriting all his wealth, including a sizeable estate near Barcino in northeast Spain. She was now a woman of substance, legally entitled to do as she wished with her newly acquired wealth.

Evander gave the ruling from the magistrate to Sabina along with another scroll.

"What is this master?"

"It is your freedom," he replied in a whisper.

Sabina thanked him again and again.

Evander continued, "I am leaving now to rejoin the Legio XX auxiliary corps."

"Stay, please, you have served more than enough years under the Eagle. If you retire now, you will be safe here in Bremetenn, and I will make sure you are well looked after in your twilight years."

"I am grateful for your offer, but I must go. The legion has been my life and I'm too old to change now. They are my brothers and the only family I've ever known".

He turned to Regulus.

"Take good care of her and be a good husband when you marry."

"I will," he said as they shook hands, "Mars protect you and victory to the twentieth."

Sabina had tears in her eyes because she was about to lose the only parent and father figure she had ever known for a second time.

"I will always carry you in my heart, please come and visit when you can."

"I promise I will when this war is over. And you must come to Deva."

"I promise. Let's hope the Brigantes sue for peace and recognise that Festus is nothing but a devious fraud who is only interested in himself."

"Perhaps, but they are a fierce people and many of them have never accepted Roman rule. I must go now and rejoin my brothers."

With that, he set off up the road to face whatever dangers might come.

"Come," said Lyra, "we should celebrate. Let's go to my apartment. Regulus, you should invite your mother, she will be most pleased that Sabina's hearing went well."

Evander walked towards the defence line on the northern ridge at a sedate pace, one foot in front of the other. He was deep in thought, memories of that day in 61CE forming up with the Legio XX to prepare for battle with Boudicca and her ferocious army of two hundred and fifty thousand Iceni and Trebantes warriors. He remembered the onslaught as the two tribes of Britannia charged up the small hill towards the lines of two Roman legions ten thousand strong, their blood curdling battle cries, and the almighty clash as they hit, the lines buckling and pushing. He remembered the screams of the dying and the wounded on both sides and how the Roman killing machine started to inexorably push forward, how the massacre began, then Boudica's army running for their lives back down the hill.

He remembered the overturned chariot with the three dead women beneath, one of them holding a newborn baby hidden under a blanket, how he had given the baby to one of the slave women in the auxiliary corps, and she had taken the baby back to Deva. He remembered the child as she grew: the bright red hair, pale white translucent skin, and green eyes. Only he, Evander, knew that the baby was the daughter of one of

Boudicca's two daughters and that as the decades and generations had passed, Sabina could trace her ancestry back to royal Iceni blood. That secret would always remain a secret and one that he, the last surviving soldier of the Legio XX who fought that day, the last man standing, would take to the grave.

Chapter Twelve
Death is Nothing to Us

The afternoon after the morning of the failed negotiations with Festus, the Legate stood atop one of the observation towers, watching enemy positions that appeared to be retreating northwards across the moorlands. He had decided against an advance that day, preferring to wait until his scouts had reported precise positions and formations of the enemy. Once he had all the information at his fingertips, he would advance using the speed and power of the Legio XX infantry and drive the enemy further into the Trough Valley towards the cavalry advancing from the other side.

On the defence line, he could see his officers and centurions were in position, ready to move at a moment's notice. Many of the soldiers were resting waiting for orders to move forward, some playing dice and gambling while others practised their swordsmanship, sparring with each other. The majority of the cavalry had been ordered eastwards along the north bank of the Belisama to the confluence of another river known as the "Stream" two miles upstream from Bremetenn. From there, they could approach the Trough Valley from the east side and, with fortune on their side, attack the enemy from the back. He was concerned that there was a risk of more Brigante reinforcements arriving from the east, but since he had not received any news to that effect, he considered the risk acceptable.

His thoughts were interrupted by one of his officers who had climbed the ladder to join him on the tower.

"Sir, two of the scouts have returned and wish to report."

"Good, tell them to meet me in my tent, I will be along shortly."

"As ordered sir."

The officer saluted and descended the ladder while the Legate continued to survey the enemy in the distance and his own defence line before descending the ladder and making his way to the command marquee. As he entered, the two scouts snapped to attention and saluted.

"Scouts, report," said the Legate.

They went to a map, which was spread across a large table, and began pointing at positions. At face value, Festus and his army were retreating towards the Trough Valley in order to pull the Roman army into a cramped position and restrict the usual three-line tactic. It was also clear that the elite of Festus's troops were heading towards the valley first so they would be the last and most effective fighters the legion would face. The Legate and his officers concluded that Festus intended to exhaust the legion fighting their way through inferior warriors only to be confronted with a tough formation of elite fighters at the back. It was not the most original tactic, but it was one that could be highly effective, especially in cramped rough terrain.

The scouts also reported that the enemy ranks had been swollen by an estimated three thousand Brigantes from the east side of the Pennine hills and a thousand from the Lonsdale tribe of the Luna valley making an army of over six thousand warriors. The Legate wanted the odds to change and he ordered the legion to stand down and wait for first light of dawn when, if reports were correct, the first cohorts of the Augusta II legion would ford the Belisama. The plan was to catch the enemy in a classic hammer and anvil tactic and box them in the Trough Valley, caught between the infantry at one end and the cavalry at the other. The officers were told to order the legion to strike camp and move forward to engage the enemy at first light.

There were those among the soldiers, who were ready for a fight, felt disappointment at having to wait another day to advance and engage the enemy. True enough, there were some battled hardened men, but a good number had only completed their training in recent years and had yet to see action. Those who had been in battles knew what it was like on the front line and they were in no hurry for the fighting to begin. They knew there was no glory in the stench and fury of fighting man to man, guts spilling, bones breaking, the ground slippery with blood. Then there was the creeping death of fevers from infected wounds and the screams of brothers in arms as limbs were amputated even as victory and glory were celebrated.

Still, the younger soldiers were eager to prove their loyalty and courage in battle for the glory of Rome and uphold the honour of the family name. All were united in their desire to put an end to the rebellion, subjugate the tribes, and have peace in Britannia. The more experienced soldiers took the extra time to rest and eat, conserving their energy for the long day ahead, knowing they would be up against a tough and fierce enemy, well known for their hatred of everything Roman.

While the Roman army rested and waited on the ridge to the north of the Belisama valley, Sabina and Lyra had returned to Lyra's apartment. Regulus had gone home to give Seren the good news about the hearing and invite her to join him at Lyra's apartment to celebrate Sabina's freedom. Despite her lack of sleep and endless workload, she had completed the linen tunic for Sabina and she brought it along to the celebration for final fitting. When the three women were together at the apartment, they disappeared into Lyra's bedroom so Sabina could try the tunic for size, all under Lyra's supervision.

Sabina came out of the bedroom and Regulus was stunned. It sat on her like she had been born to wear it, her usual wild map of hair tamed in plaits and pinned around her head in the Roman style, rouge on her lips, and a brilliant white line tunic that stopped just above her knees. A new pair of black leather sandals, fashioned from spare leather by Seren, completed the outfit. She looked every inch ready to take her place as a Freedwoman of Rome, ready to be educated under Lyra's tutelage, which Lyra had promised would continue even though she was no longer a slave.

All Regulus could do was wonder how he was ever going to believe his good fortune, shape up, and keep up. It was not just Lyra who thought that there was something about Sabina. Regulus sensed it too and he had to smile at the fact that it was not two weeks ago that she was a grime covered slave at Portus Piscium out in the Belisama estuary.

"Do you like it?" she asked.

"I love it, and you look like you were born to wear it."

Lyra began to fuss about.

"It could do with taking in a bit here, perhaps loosening off a bit there."

"I will see to it tomorrow," said Seren as she made careful notes.

"Excellent," said Lyra, "and now we shall have food and wine."

Sabina went back into Lyra's bedroom to change, reluctant to go back to her drab grey tunic that she associated with being a slave. She was still in a state of shock at the outcome of the hearing, knowing how close she had come to disaster and certain death. Deep down, she knew how precarious life could be under Roman rule. Even the Emperor needed constant protection from murderous plots and assassination attempts. She also felt it was a little premature to celebrate until the war with Festus and the northern Britannia tribes had been settled. She was in no doubt what would happen if Festus and the Brigantes were victorious. Suicide would be the best option in that event. But just as she had calculated before her escape, she was sure that the legions would prevail.

For now, all she could do was accept the good things and people that fortune had laid out before her and enjoy her newfound freedom. After all, who knew what the gods had in store for mere mortals such as her in this life before crossing over into the afterlife. So she changed and went out to the main room to join the others, who had been joined by Astrid. Lyra had laid out food and drink so everything was in its correct place: olives, salmon, venison, bread, oil, fish sauce, all in separate wooden bowls and a large earthenware jug of wine. Everyone ate and drank heartily, the conversation dominated by Sabina's freedom and her forthcoming marriage to Regulus. For his part, Regulus felt somewhat out of place, unable to get a word in edgeways.

The topic of war and the imminent threat of a battle to the north of Bremetenn was studiously ignored and for now they were all happy for it to be so. There was joy and laughter to be had and much to celebrate in the moment, although Astrid became tearful at one point because she had received no word about Marcellus. Regulus was able to offer some consolation by telling her that he was in charge of things at Arma Officinas, alive and well the last time he had seen him.

The celebrations continued into early evening when Regulus excused himself on the grounds of having to take a watch with his rowers and ensure the *Belisama Cygnus* was ready for battle if an order was given. Sabina walked to the door with him.

"I hope you will not have to fight tomorrow."

"Don't worry Sabina, we've both been through worse than this. In any event the Legio XX are here and the Brigantes will never breach their defences."

"You will be careful, won't you?"

Regulus grinned, "You're beginning to sound like my mother."

"Hmm, don't be so flippant, she cares about you too."

"I'm teasing. In any case, I have much to live for so I'm in no hurry to take unnecessary risks."

"I'm glad to hear it. I'll see you when this stupid war is over and may all the gods protect you."

"And you, I shall see you soon."

He left the apartment and walked down to the riverbank, down the steps, and onto the loading dock. His thoughts strayed to the memory of that day with Gabo when he took his first trial command and the speed of his assent to full command dictated by a few days of events. He was now caught up in a time of war, a grown man about to marry and, perhaps, sooner rather than later, start a family of his own with Sabina. He wanted peace and in that, begin to develop a new era of trade and prosperity on the river. But for now, he knew he must focus on being a servant of Rome unto death in a time of war.

Dadas was busy replacing two worn leather grips on the oars. He popped up from behind one of the shields and acknowledged Regulus.

"It seems the fighting is not yet done."

Regulus looked skyward.

"Ever it seems to be."

"Perhaps the legions will finish the job fast."

"I would not want to be a Brigante rebel tonight. The legions are merciless once they get started."

"They are indeed, and Festus will be made to answer for his treachery."

"One way or another, even if I have to do the job myself."

Dadas changed the subject.

"I hear Sabina has been given her freedom by her rightful owner."

"She has, so at last we will be able to marry."

"I have nothing but joy for you both – at least I can look forward to a good wedding."

Regulus laughed, "If we survive this war."

"Shall I take the first watch?"

"Get some rest," replied Regulus, "I'm wide awake and more than happy to do it."

Regulus went aboard the boat to consult the tide tabulations as Dadas settled under a waterproof cover. He knew the tides were now at their lowest, the half-moon in the sky correlating with his tabulations. It would not be possible to carry much weight into the tidal reaches of the river even at high water. Any military action would have to be confined to the upper section of the river close to Bremetenn. He satisfied himself that everything was in order on the boat and settled down himself for the four-hour watch with two guards on the loading dock for company.

Up on the ridge, the campfires along the defence line crackled and blazed sending sparks up into the darkness and lighting up the weather-beaten faces of the men of the Legio XX, each man knowing that tomorrow could be his last day. And for many of them, the words of Lucretius that, "death is nothing to us" offered comfort, resolve, and courage in the face of perils to come.

Out on the moorlands to the north of the Roman defence line, Festus and his Brigante chiefs supervised the retreat towards the Trough Valley. Festus's fellow Roman collaborators had trained the Brigantes in how to follow a chain of command and form up in blocks in an organised fashion, although some of the Brigantes seemed to be unwilling to follow orders, which made the Romans liken the task to "herding cats". As the retreat continued, a scout rode into camp and reported to Festus.

"Sir, it's how you said it would be. The Roman cavalry are riding on the road following the Stream. Just like you said, infantry at the west entrance and cavalry coming round the back."

"Excellent, they have fallen for it," said Festus with deep self-satisfaction.

"They have sir."

"Keep monitoring the situation. I want reports from every location on the Stream and in the Trough Valley every hour."

Festus turned to his Brigante chiefs.

"Maintain the slow move towards the Trough Valley. I want the Legio XX Legate to believe that is where we intend to accept battle. Wait until just before dawn and then we shall goad them forward. Once we have them in position, we shall counter-attack."

"The cavalry will be useless and stuck in the Trough Valley…"

"Trying to defend against skirmishers and guerrilla attacks from the hills slowing them down," interrupted Festus.

"Hit and run tactics," said one of the Brigante chiefs.

"Exactly," said Festus.

They rode off leaving Festus alone with his thoughts. He was determined to inflict as much damage as possible on his old legion, driven by vengeance and hatred for the way he had been undermined and given such a paltry token Prefecture at Portus Piscium. He was also keen to get back to, and expand, his business interests: stealing and trafficking slaves. And once he had smashed the Legio XX, he would be the de facto ruler of confederate states in northern Britannia. The last thing on his mind was how many were going to die in the name of his twisted ambitions.

Chapter Thirteen
Hammer and Anvil

Birdsong greeted the pre-dawn morning, filling the air with sweet sound as the birds went about their business on the moorland, oblivious to the two armies facing off against each other. Mars was in full ascendency giving the only clue to the violence of war that was about to unfold. A faint violet glow in the east heralded the advent of daybreak.

Cyrus had been awake on watch for two hours, conscious of his responsibilities as Primus Pilus to the cohort made up of the four hundred and eighty legionaries, which he knew would be in the front line of battle and liable to take the highest number of casualties. Far from his native Syria for the past twenty years of service in the Legio XX, he still marvelled at the green and fertile world of Britannia, which contrasted so much against the dry and baked landscape where he grew up as a boy. Unlike some in the legion who cursed the cold and wet climate, he felt at one with the natural world and grateful for an endless water supply. He knew from firsthand experience how cruel drought could be, unforgiving days without clean water under a relentless blistering sun.

He marched up and down the defence line, watching for any movement that could signify a night assault, or any change in enemy positions, checking the other guards on watch had not fallen asleep at their posts or decided to run away, although such incidents were rare since punishments were brutal and often fatal. He paused his marching to look out over the landscape and noticed a darker patch of moorland appeared to have moved. He rubbed his eyes and looked again, doubting his senses, and decided to climb up one of the observation towers and check from a different angle. When he reached the top, he ordered the soldier on duty to look out.

"Soldier, look over there," pointing in the direction of the dark patch, "what do you see?"

"Primus Pilus, I'm not sure, but look towards the direction of the Trough Valley entrance. It looks like a block of land is shifting slightly – I don't know, perhaps it's the twilight of dawn playing tricks on my eyes."

"Perhaps, but that is what I saw too."

Another guard shouted up to them from below.

"Brothers, look over there," he said pointing in the same direction, "it looks like something is afoot."

Then they saw another block in the distance moving in their direction, the increasing light of dawn making the movement more visible. Cyrus descended the ladder, ran to the command marquee, and demanded that the guard wake the Legate as a matter of extreme urgency. The Legate stumbled to the entrance of the tent, still half asleep.

"Yes, what is it Primus Pilus?"

"Sir, please come with me. It looks like the enemy is advancing towards us, crawling on the ground under cover of twilight."

"Are you sure?"

"Please, Legate, come and see for yourself."

They mounted the observation tower and the Legate looked out into the distance. What he saw convinced him. The enemy was advancing in short bursts, organised in blocks, blending into the moorland grass and heather, difficult to see even though the sun was starting to show from behind the Pennine Hills to the east of them. The Legate reached for the bell and rang the alarm.

Within ten minutes all the cohorts had formed up into battle formation blocks of eighty legionaries, the centurions shouting orders, steel and iron clashing, archers in position, catapults and ballista machines manned and loaded, auxiliaries armed with bows and spears ready to act as skirmishers to harass the enemy around the edges of the battlefield. And as the sun began to cast his rays from the east, Festus's army began to advance faster, increasing the tempo in lockstep with the beat of war drums as they came closer to the Roman lines. Then they came to a halt just short of the Roman defence line and stayed out of range of the catapults and archers.

The Romans were surprised by the discipline and organisation of Festus's army, marshalled in blocks with spaces between them, mirroring the legionary tactic of allowing fresh warriors to swap places with tired ones on the front line. There was also the disconcerting fact that the Roman cavalry was nowhere to be seen. The Legio XX were outnumbered facing a fierce enemy, and a hard gruelling fight. The younger recruits, who had been so eager to fight and prove their valour, did not now appear to be quite so enthusiastic.

The Legate gave the order and auxiliaries flung wooden bridges across the defence ditches. Each century marched across and formed up in battle formation on the other side, a long line at the front and blocks behind. The speed and discipline with which the Romans deployed dazzled the Brigantes, but, undeterred, they clashed their swords and axes on their shields in time with the war drums issuing battle cries and chants, taunting the Romans to advance and engage in battle, threatening to annihilate them in combat. On the Roman side, trumpets sounded in short sequential bursts, each sequence coded for manoeuvring a certain way, short whistles sounding within each century relaying orders from the centurions. When the Romans were set in formation, they fell stone silent. They were ready.

One long blast on the trumpets signified the order to advance and the front line charged. The Brigantes charged forward in response, but before the two armies met, another trumpet blast ordered the Romans to stop and throw their spears, each spear finding its mark in a warrior, or embedded in a shield rendering it cumbersome and useless. Then the Romans drew their swords, shields up, soldiers shoulder to shoulder in tight formation, forward at the quickstep until they clashed with the enemy blocks. The slaughter began, the whistles blew, trumpets blaring signals, each man fighting one on one at the front, relieved regularly by a fresh man waiting behind.

The Romans had positioned themselves in such a way as to allow themselves room to retreat a few paces at a time so the front line could bow inwards, little by little in the middle. The Brigantes had failed to notice the ploy, and, sensing they had found a weak spot, began to push harder. They failed to notice two Roman blocks of troops, one on each side behind the battleline lying in wait and, worse still, that they were being drawn into range of the Roman war machines and archers. Festus, familiar with the tactic from his time with the Legio XX, screamed orders at the Brigante chiefs to pull their warriors back. It was too late. Roman archers fired over their comrades finding their marks in the Brigante ranks with the war machines deploying their payloads with devastating results. The Roman front line broke, allowing hundreds of Brigante warriors to burst through, only to be met by a corridor of death from the two Roman blocks waiting behind. Panic began to take hold in the Brigante ranks.

As the sun swung higher in the sky, the relentless fighting and slaughter increased in ferocity, appalling wounds and death inflicted on both sides. What the Brigantes lacked in organisation they made up for with fierce courage and skill with their weapons as they fought on, but the Romans fought with great valour, well-rehearsed battle tactics, and years of training, increasing the pressure on Festus's army despite being outnumbered.

It was then that the first two cohorts of the Augusta II arrived, bolstering the Legio XX with fresh troops, ready to join the battle. They were ordered to attack the flanks of the Brigantes further boxing them in, so Festus gave the order to deploy his elite warriors who had been waiting at the back until ordered to charge in and join the fighting. They smashed into the Romans with such force that the lines buckled and, in some spots, gave way. Festus shouted words of encouragement, the Brigante chiefs egging their warriors on and jumping into battle with them as they began to make headway, inflicting losses on the Roman side as they pushed forward sensing that they were turning the tide.

A third block of Romans advanced and plugged the gap where a Brigante breakthrough looked likely to succeed, and as they did so, another cohort of Augusta II had arrived and joined the fray. Auxiliaries, sensing the rising tempo of the battle skirmished around the edges firing arrows at the Brigantes, employing "hit and run" tactics. The Brigante elite fighters, even as they continued to wreak havoc in the Roman lines, began to take significant losses and the Brigante numerical superiority diminished in what had fast become a battle of blood-soaked attrition.

The Legate and his officers ran around at the back of the battle lines issuing orders, trumpets sounding the codes for the centurions to wheel their men round, attack, withdraw, and relieve. The slick Roman manoeuvres caused confusion in the Brigante ranks and in some positions, a sense of panic began to take hold as some found themselves in a desperate fight for survival.

The killer blow in favour of the Romans came from an unlikely source. Decimus had been warned by a Roman scout to return to support the Legio XX and told about how Festus had duped the Romans into believing that the site of battle would be in the Trough Valley. Decimus had relied on intelligence received and ordered the cavalry to return back down the Stream Road to Bremetenn and so on up to the defence line.

Decimus looked at the battlefield and did not need to wait for an order from the Legate or his officers to know what needed to be done. He led his cavalry in a wide arc around the enemy blocks until he was in position at their back, far enough away to form a long line formation. Then he gave the order to charge, and the cavalry, at full gallop, spears at the ready, advanced towards the back of Festus's army. The Legate saw what was happening and committed all his troops to advance at the front and catch the Brigantes in a classic hammer and anvil manoeuvre.

It worked. The cavalry smashed into the back of the battle, causing panic and disorder, Roman spears finding their mark, Brigante warriors trampled under the horses hooves, and sent flying by the impact. Horses and men began to suffer terrible injuries. Casualties on both sides began to mount, but now the tables had turned, and the Brigantes found themselves outnumbered and outmanoeuvred. All their hopes and dreams of reclaiming their lands and enjoying an era of peace and prosperity within a confederation of tribes began to fade and die with them on a blood-soaked battlefield, but still they fought on, refusing to surrender to Roman rule.

However hard the Brigantes fought their efforts became more futile. Now, the Romans closed in from all sides and the Brigantes found themselves trapped in a killing zone. One by one, some of them began to throw down weapons and surrender while others fought on, preferring to die on feet, sword in hand in the spirit of being true warriors until the last gasp.

Prisoners were seized and each one was chained to a long chain a yard apart from the next. Those who were considered unfit because of their wounds were executed on the spot. Slave drivers and merchants from the auxiliaries came forward to oversee the process of their new "stock", arguing amongst themselves about prices, some trying to find a bargain gladiator to train for the arena, others looking for attractive women and girls in the Brigante baggage train. The chained Brigantes sat, disarmed, and exhausted, wondering what fate had in store. They soon found out as they were ordered to stand and face the Legio XX Legate.

"You have been defeated and you are now slaves of the Senate and People of Rome. It is a price you must pay for breaking the Pax Romana. You will be forced marched north under the guard of the Legio XX until you reach the Stanegate Road. Once there, you will quarry stone for our glorious Emperor Hadrian's project to set the northern border of Britannia once and for all. Any attempt to escape and the cross awaits you. Your rebellion is over. A full pardon and freedom will be granted to any man who gives me the whereabouts of the traitor, Festus Crassus. To the rest, be glad your lives have been spared. Hail Ceasar!"

He stepped aside and issued an order for the battlefield to be scoured for Festus and to kill any enemy warriors who might be playing dead. A full year's pay was promised to any soldier who found Festus, insisting that he must be taken alive.

Meanwhile, Decimus staggered about the battlefield wondering how he was still alive and unscathed after leading the cavalry charge. He had lost many brothers from the Bremetenn and Mamucium cavalry. He stayed on his feet despite an overwhelming feeling of exhaustion after all the fighting, driven by his determination to find Festus and drag him to justice for his murderous treachery. As he searched, Roman physicians and their slave assistants triaged those from the legions who could be saved and manned stretchers for those who could not walk back to tents, which had been set up as a battlefield infirmary. He was saddened to find the body of Primus Pilus Cyrus, killed in the first attack as he led his cohort into battle.

But his spirits were lifted by the sight of Marcellus coming towards him.

"Marcellus, brother, you are well met – what are you doing here?"

"Primus Pilus Decimus, how in the name of Mars are you still alive after leading that cavalry charge?"

"I have no idea," he said shrugging his shoulders, "perhaps the afterlife was full and I must die another day."

"All the gods have smiled on you today."

"Anyway, why are you here and not at Arma Officinas?"

"Arma Officinas is now under the charge of the Legio XX so I was granted leave to return to Bremetenn. I came over here with the first cohort of the Augusta II."

"I see, well I'm searching for that treacherous scum, Festus Crassus."

"All hands to the pump with that one, the Legio XX have seconded me to help organise the roadblocks. Everything and every person is to be searched and questioned."

A messenger from the Legate came over and addressed Decimus.

"Primus Pilus Decimus, you are to report to the Legate immediately."

"I will, as ordered."

Marcellus smiled, "On personal terms with the Legate. Onwards and upwards to glory."

"No stopping me now brother," quipped Decimus, "I shall see you back in Bremetenn, that is if he doesn't have me executed for leading an unauthorised cavalry charge."

"Mars protect you."

"And you."

Decimus walked to the Legate's command marquee as fast as he could, wondering why he had been summoned. He hoped that it was nothing to do with his spontaneous cavalry charge. Given the circumstances, he could not see how he could have acted otherwise. True, he had lost many good men in the fury of battle, but that was always a hazard in war, ordered or not. He entered the tent, stood to attention, and saluted.

"Legate, sir, you ordered me to report."

"Yes, Primus Pilus, I did. You ordered a cavalry charge without authority. Explain yourself."

"Sir, had it not been for one of our scouts getting word to me, I would be at the east side entrance to the Trough Valley wondering where everyone was. I returned here based on intelligence received. Given the battle was in progress when I arrived, with you and your officers fully engaged giving orders to the infantry, I acted the best I could given the situation. With all respect, I stand by my decision and accept full responsibility."

"I see," said the Legate, pausing for a second, "you do realise I could decimate your unit and have you flogged for acting without orders and insubordination?"

"I do, and I still stand firm."

"Very well, since that is your final word, I am commending you for your courage, initiative, and sound leadership. It is my error of judgement that sent you on an erroneous mission in the first place."

Decimus was taken aback, unsure of what to say so he told himself that usually meant it was better to say nothing.

"What do you have to say for yourself?"

"I am indeed humbled and honoured sir."

"Good man. Now, I am ordering half the Legio XX to march north to the Stanegate Road to begin preparations for Emperor Hadrian's border project. A good number of your Asturian Cavalry will accompany them. Do you wish to command and lead them?"

"Sir, I am honoured by such an offer, however I am due to retire and I would like to oversee the rebuilding of Bremetennacum battlements in stone and breed first rate horses."

"I see. Well, you certainly deserve it after your loyal service."

"Thank you, sir, I am most grateful."

"Perhaps, now that Sextus has passed into the afterlife, you would consider the position of Prefect, which would encompass Bremetennacum, Portus Piscium, and the Hill Fort?"

Decimus paused for thought before replying. He hated administrative duties, but then he thought of Lyra and the Fort Clerk. The Fort Clerk could handle the accounts and stock checks, and Lyra was more than capable of handling all the administrative and legal duties. Lyra was also capable of handling the niceties of entertaining any official visits and her skills of interrogation were without question if needed.

"By my honour, I accept."

"Excellent, my clerk will draw up the scroll of office. I will seal it and have it delivered to you today."

"I am honoured to serve, er, may I ask how things are to the east of the Pennine Hills?"

"Yes, the Legio VI have pushed the Caledonians to the north of the Stanegate Road and the plan is to keep them there with a set border according to Emperor Hadrian's design. The northern tribes of Britannia are divided with the Brigantes broken and defeated."

"The end of Festus's rebellion."

"We think so, although Festus is still at large at least one barbarian chief is missing with him. In the context of being a figurehead, he still represents a threat, but it remains doubtful as whether or not he could raise another army. Still, he must be found and brought to justice. Dismissed".

Decimus left and went to find Marcellus who he found overseeing a roadblock.

"Marcellus, the Legate has made me Prefect of Bremetenn."

"Commiserations brother," said Marcellus.

"...and I want to make you Primus Pilus of the cavalry."

Marcellus's smile dropped as fast as it had been raised.

"Sir," he said as he snapped to attention and saluted, "I am honoured and by my honour and Mars I accept."

"Good, no better man for the job. I'll have a formal scroll of office delivered to you as soon as possible. I assume you're still looking for Festus here?"

"Legate's orders."

"I thought the Brigante chiefs would have given him up by now."

"Nothing so far, but they will soon change their minds. They are to be executed one by one in front of each other until one of them starts talking."

"I see, report to me at Bremetenn when you have discharged your orders here."

"Yes, Prefect Decimus."

Decimus could not help feeling some regret about what was about to happen to the Brigante chiefs. True, they had broken the Pax Romana and participated in a murderous rebellion that had killed and maimed so many of his brothers in arms. But they were courageous warriors who had fought for their ancestral homeland and as such, he did not think they deserved the humiliation and physical vandalism about to be inflicted upon them. Better to sentence them to the arena where could at least die with some honour, fighting and dying with sword in hand as a true warrior should.

He looked down, shook his head, turned and mounted his horse to ride back to Bremetenn and assume his position as a Prefect of the Roman Empire.

Chapter Fourteen
Money Matters

At the fort, Decimus was greeted by a cheering crowd of the cavalry, many still blooded from battle, who wanted to show their gratitude to him for a great victory and putting down a dangerous rebellion. Swords waved over their heads, glinting in the torchlight as the last rays of daylight began to fade. They cheered again and again at the tops of their voices, and Decimus felt overcome by the euphoria of triumph among the men under his command. He dismounted his horse, again wondering how he had managed to survive. Regulus, Sabina, Seren, and Astrid stood with other villagers at the north entrance to the fort cheering and applauding the great victory, which had liberated Bremetenn from the threat of destruction.

Decimus made his way through the crowd to his new quarters, feeling out of place in his new post as Prefect, which seemed surreal. He half-expected to see Sextus appear to greet him and when he did enter his new quarters, he was surprised to see Lyra stood waiting for him with the clerk of the fort sat to one side, stylus, and wax tablet in hand.

"Decimus, thank the gods you are victorious and unharmed," said Lyra in her warmest of voice.

"I thank you, and I am glad you are well too."

"I have managed to keep things in order here, although I grieve for Sextus."

"I too grieve for our fallen Prefect, but for now we must cling to matters at hand now I have been appointed to the post of Prefect of Bremetenn."

"I congratulate you Prefect Decimus. How may I be of service?"

"Administration of the fort and village. Also, I want you to continue in your role as interrogator."

"I am honoured and it is my pleasure to serve."

"Good. Now, how are the food and grain stocks?"

"Not good. Many of the deliverers are overdue. The disruption to trade and supplies on the roads and the Belisama have put us in a precarious position. Hosting a cohort of the Legio XX added to the drain of resources."

"I see, well, we will have to impose rationing in the fort and village."

"As you command," said Lyra in her most formal voice, "and what do we know of Festus's whereabouts?"

"Still at large."

"Ah, I see. No doubt he will be apprehended soon."

"I would think so. The rebellion has been crushed – a matter of when not if. What news from here?"

"I almost forgot," said Lyra with a nonchalant air, "the missing chest has been found."

"Found!?"

"Indeed. Two slaves from the bath house furnace room were out in the woods chopping wood for the furnace when they happened upon it, half buried behind a bush. They brought it here immediately."

Decimus was stunned.

"How do we know it wasn't them that stole it in the first place and then lost their nerve?"

"I checked their movements," said Lyra, flat as a tabletop, "they were on furnace duty the night the chest went missing. All the slaves were working at the double because of the demand for bathing from the men of the Legio XX."

"Still seems odd to me."

"I understand your suspicion. In any event, I now own the chest."

"What are you talking about; it belongs to the emperor."

"Actually – and forgive me for saying so – it belonged to the Prefect of the fort because it is a spoil of war."

"Well, then it passes to me in my new role as Prefect."

"Ah, but you handed it in to Sextus before he died. Therefore, Sextus had legal ownership. Sextus left me everything in his Will, and that includes the chest."

"I think not. You are not a Roman citizen and you need to be in order to make that claim."

"I was coming that, you see, Sextus made me a citizen of Rome in his Will."

Decimus exploded with frustration.

"I demand to see the Will!"

"Of course, I have it here – somewhere – ahh, here it is," she said as she rummaged about with scrolls on the table.

Decimus muttered to himself as he read the Will. It was authentic and, as Lyra had pointed out, everything that was his was now hers. He handed the Will back to Lyra, who was the first to speak.

"Prefect Decimus, if I may, I have a commerce proposition for you."

"And what commerce proposition is that?"

"I am willing to invest in the future prosperity of Bremetenn."

"Invest in what way?"

"First, I want to finance new horse breeding stock. Second, I want to finance the river economy, and third, assist in any outlay needed to refurbish the wooden battlements on the fort ramparts with stone."

"All those are laudable ambitions, but what do you want in return?"

"A simple interest return on a rolling annual basis. My main motivation is to bring prosperity to Bremetenn."

"Continue."

"We must do this to rebuild relations with the tribes and continue to Romanise as many as possible. The Brigantes and the Setantii must be shown that they can prosper within the Roman Empire just like the tribes in the south of Britannia."

"That will not be easy. What is left of the Brigantes is either being dragged north in chains to work and die in the stone quarries preparing for Emperor Hadrian's great wall project, or nailed to crosses screaming the sky down."

"True, but there are others who did not participate in the rebellion: women, children, many of the hill farmers that could be encouraged to adopt the Roman way."

"Write the plans down and give the proposed tabulations to the fort clerk. I want to inspect everything and make sure that you do not do this just to serve your own purposes."

"Of course. In the meantime, please allow me to suggest that you look at the clerk's tabulations for Bremetenn's financial state. You will find there is no money on hand to pay for things, including the soldiers' pay."

"What!?"

"I'm afraid so. Sextus was a wonderful Prefect in the military context, but he missed opportunities to grow the economy of the land under his control. Things just about got done and paid for on a day-to-day basis, but the rebellion has turned things upside down."

Decimus began to think he had become Prefect of a liability, but he was still sceptical of Lyra's proposition. The chest, the finances, the Will – coincidence or conspiracy? And he certainly disliked the fact that he would be beholden to Lyra as far as money was concerned. He decided to wait, get all the facts on the table, and investigate further.

"Very well, I will look at the accounts and your proposals. For now, you are dismissed."

"As you command Prefect Decimus," said Lyra as she bowed and floated out of the room.

"Guard, bring me the two slaves from the furnace room who found the chest."

"At once Prefect Decimus."

The two slaves were marched before Decimus who addressed them with menace in his voice:

"Now, you two slaves will tell me the truth. Were you involved in a plot to steal the chest?"

The slaves looked terrified as one of them spoke in a shaky voice.

"No Prefect Decimus, we were on wood detail for furnace fuel – the demand you see – we saw the chest sticking out of the ground. Whoever tried to hide it did a bad job. We brought it here. Handed it over to Lyra without any delay."

"I think you stole the chest and lost your nerve."

"By all the gods, no, I swear – just wanted to do the right thing."

"It's what we did, we're not thieves Prefect Decimus, we are loyal slaves to Bremetenn and the Roman Empire," offered the second slave.

Decimus sat back and fixed the two slaves in his gaze. They stood in front of him, heads bowed, hands clasped, frozen to the spot and shaking with fear. Both slaves were long serving at the bath house and neither had ever put a foot wrong. Still, Decimus thought about torturing them, but pushed the thought away, knowing that they would tell him anything. Under different circumstances, this would be a job for Lyra and her clever interrogation techniques, but since he suspected her of being in on the whole thing, that was not an option.

"Go back to your duties slaves, but do not think this is the end of the matter."

They let out a gasp of relief as the prospect of interrogation receded. They saluted and left the Prefect's chambers in a hurry as Decimus began to read the financial tabulations of Bremetenn, which, as Lyra had pointed out, did not paint a prosperous picture. What he read told him he had taken charge of a broke Prefecture, with no hope of a cash input in the short term, and nothing for any investment in longer term prosperity. The fort clerk looked at him with a stark expression of resignation.

"Prefect Decimus," said the clerk glumly, "what would you have me do?"

"It does seem like Lyra's proposal is perhaps the way to get things back on track for now and in the future."

"It does. Shall I send word for her to return?"

"Yes, have the guard bring her over and tell her to wait here for my return. In the meantime, I must deal with the Setantii hostages."

"Immediately sir!"

Decimus entered a section of the barracks where the hostages were being held under guard. Downcast and bedraggled, they had been told that the legions had crushed the rebellion and the hostages could only speculate what was in store for them. Execution or slavery were both possibilities, especially as they had been told what had happened to the Brigantes. Decimus was emphatic about the terms of peace as he addressed the warrior who he had negotiated with at Arma Officinas.

"Setantii, you will be freed to lead your people in a peaceful and mutually beneficial relationship under Roman rule. You will provide labour to assist in the reconstruction of the Hill Fort to make good on the damage you have caused. Both your elders will be executed for colluding with a treacherous Roman, insurrection, and breaking the Pax Romana – guards take them away and execute them now!"

The Setantii elders were dragged outside, both protesting that they were sacred and how the Druid priests would seek revenge for such an outrage before both were silenced.

"Warrior, do we have an agreement?"

"We do," said the warrior, "you have my word, I will sign for the Setantii and lead them forward to prosperity and peaceful co-operation."

"Good," said Decimus with authority, "any breach of the agreement and you will find Rome is not so accommodating a second time."

"I understand and again, I give you my word of honour."

"Let us move forward and restore trade between Bremetenn and Portus Piscium."

Decimus freed the hostages and returned to his quarters to find Lyra waiting. He sat down and looked her straight in the eye, and although he tried to fight it, he could not help but be amazed by her poise and elegance; statuesque with a presence that filled the room and wrapped around him like a warm blanket. He wondered what it was about this woman that was so hypnotic and persuasive. Whatever it was, he decided to harness the power and use it before it used him. He was not the first man to assume he could do so.

"I have spoken to the two slaves and, for now, I am prepared to accept their explanation. But, if anything points to an attempted robbery, they will face justice as will anyone else who may have been involved."

Lyra replied with honey dripping from her voice.

"Of course, Prefect Decimus, and as interrogator, I would be only too happy to assist you as required."

"Very well, I shall expect you to draft a document outlining your proposals. If I approve, we can arrange a hearing with the magistrate and ensure that everything complies with Roman law."

"I shall begin work right away."

"Good, however the soldiers' pay must come from state coffers. I shall send word to Governor Falco to have the necessary funds transferred as soon as possible. The soldiers will no doubt grumble, but they know I am a man of my word so they will wait."

"As you command."

"It seems we have much to do."

"We do, and, um, there is something else if you can spare a moment."

"What is it?"

"It concerns Sabina."

"What about that impudent slave woman?"

"Well, she is now a Freedwoman."

"I see, another surprise and, um, how was that one arranged?"

Lyra explained what had happened with Evander arriving at Bremetenn with the Legio XX, the hearing with the magistrate, and Evander giving Sabina her freedom. Decimus sat dumbfounded, and began to think that he would have to have a conversation with Regulus.

Lyra went on.

"The thing is, Sabina is happy to carry on working for me in exchange for her education."

"To what end does she wish be educated?"

"She could be excellent as a go between for peaceful assimilation of the tribes and the land under your control. She is fluent in the coastal dialect of the Setantii thanks to her years of slavery at Portus Piscium, and she is capable when speaking and understanding Celtic. Under my tutelage, she is learning Latin at a fast rate – she is quick and eager to learn."

Decimus shifted in his chair as the bruises sustained in battle began to ache.

"What, by all the gods, is it about this woman that is so keen to be Romanised?"

"I can't say for certain, but I think it is her curiosity that drives her. And I think that she sees order and education as the way forward for the well-being and prosperity for the people of Britannia."

"I agree we must keep the peace with the tribes, but really, this ex-slave woman?"

"I think so. And there is something else about her – how can I put this – she seems, well, born to lead."

"She has some cahonis, but what makes you think she has leadership qualities?"

"In short, I do not know. Perhaps it is her charisma and energy."

"You could have said that about Boudica and she caused all sorts of problems."

"I think Boudica had rather different motivations and ambitions."

"I must think on all this with care."

"Of course, but I do not think Emperor Hadrian will be pleased by this latest episode of violence and disruption in Britannia."

"I agree, he will be most displeased and I suspect Governor Falco will be moved on and replaced. The emperor wants peace, prosperity, and Greek style culture within set borders. The days of conquest and expansion of the empire are over."

"Then may I venture to say that it is all the more imperative to bring about peace and prosperity to persuade the tribes, especially the Brigantes, to reject reckless rebellions and treacherous renegades like Festus Crassus."

"I will think on. In the meantime, we must press on as there is much to do. Dismissed!"

"As you command."

The guard ushered Lyra out, returned, and stood to attention.

"Prefect Decimus, if I may."

"Yes, what is it?" snapped Decimus.

"Apologies, but there is a woman called Seren here to see you."

"Juno protect me from women and politicians!"

"Shall I send her away?"

"No, no, show her in."

Seren entered Decimus's quarters with her head bowed and she cradled a sack of something in her arms. He gestured for her to take a seat and offered her a cup of wine, remembering common civilities, pushing back against his grumpy mood, and the pain of the bruises which aggravated him. There was also the fact that he still had a soft spot for Seren, which always surprised him, even after all the years that had passed since their brief summer of romance. Her calm and considered manner seemed to bring a sense of peace to his fighting spirit.

"Seren, I hope you are well?"

Seren looked up at the Prefect and natural father of her son.

"I am well, and I am pleased to see you well and unharmed after all the fighting."

"I thank you. How may I be of service?"

"It is this," she said as she produced a copper helmet with a mask from the sack.

Decimus starred at the tranquil godlike face of the mask, stunned by its intricate and delicate design.

"Where on earth did you find that?"

It was in a chest that Gabo bequeathed to me in his Will."

"Why have you brought it to me?"

"Because here is a letter from Gabo – he wants it to go to a Roman warrior who has gone above and beyond the call of duty in the service of Rome."

"As he did on the Rhine during those blood-soaked campaigns against Germania."

"And when he saved your life."

"I have never forgotten my debt of gratitude to Gabo. Had it not been for him, I, and many of my brothers in arms would be at the bottom of the Rhine."

If Gabo were here now, he would tell you how he blessed the day he was of service to you and the Legio XX, crossing the river under hails of arrows to save you from the German side."

"I've had some narrow escapes in my time, but I will never forget that day. Our failed bridgehead forced into retreat with the mighty river in full flood at our backs, Gabo piloting the boat across to rescue us. If ever a man deserved to wear a parade mask for courage and honour, it was Gabo for his actions that day."

"And I think he will rejoice in the afterlife if you now accept the honour."

"With all my heart, I will."

"I am so pleased. Now, may I ask you to give your blessing to the union of Regulus and Sabina?"

"Yes, and I will speak with Regulus very soon. It seems I must now accept that Sabina is no longer a slave."

"Now, I am sure you have much to do in your new role as Prefect of Bremetenn."

"I do."

Seren readied herself to leave.

"I would be pleased if you might call for supper sometime."

"I would like to accept your gracious offer – perhaps when food deliveries begin to flow again and the rationing is over."

"Of course, and it will be good to see the back of these troubled times."

"Guard, escort the lady out of the fort and make sure she has all she needs."

"Sir!"

It was only then that Decimus realised he was covered in spilled Brigante blood.

Out in the Trough Valley, deep inside, hidden by bushes, something stirred; something that burned with vengeance and hatred, full of wounded greed and entitlement; something that was selling its soul to the four Furies of Hades at any price they may see fit to set; something that was human, yet devoid of all humanity. That something was Festus Crassus.

Chapter Fifteen
White Wedding

Twenty-nine days had passed since Sabina's desperate escape from Portus Piscium. She stood outside Lyra's apartment staring at the moon under a cloudless night sky remembering how the night of her escape had changed her life in every way she had dreamed possible. She pointed at the base of the moon without thinking, drawn by its inexplicable gravity as it pulled and dragged the sea, flooding the marshes and covering everything in its path just as it had covered everything behind her and aided her flight from captivity. Now, here she was on the eve of her marriage to Regulus in Bremetenn, the place she had begun to call home and where she hoped her children would grow up strong and free Roman citizens. And she hoped that peace would reign with no more war and all its inherent violence and cruelty.

The cold air of the night began to seep into her bones as she realised she had come outside without a cloak, but still she stared up at the moon and wondered what it was that fascinated her so much. She had questioned Lyra during a tutorial about why it waxed and waned and why it had such power over the sea. Lyra could only offer that things happened that way and because it was natural, it was an end in and of itself, so it must be good and we humans must learn to live in tune with that which happens "of nature".

She moved about a little, folding her arms about herself in an effort to keep warm. Then a warm cloak was unexpectedly draped around her as Lyra appeared, holding her close and dispelling the cold. Neither spoke for a few moments as they both sensed the bond between them. Sabina felt the pull of attraction and the guilt that came with it. Lyra sensed the effect she had on Sabina, but she also felt this would be the last time they would share a quiet moment together. The morning would see Sabina and Regulus made one and Lyra felt something deep inside that she only felt on rare occasions: lonely, aided and abetted by the fact that Decimus had told her that Cyrus had been killed while fighting in the final battle with the rebels.

Sabina was the first to break the silence.

"I am sorry for disturbing you. My old habits die hard."

"It is of no consequence, I understand."

"Things have been so overwhelming. So much has happened these past twenty-nine days."

"You could say things have been rather eventful."

"You have a talent for understatement."

"Ah, well, there's no sense in getting all worked up about things. One should keep a cool head – anyway, you should be happy, tomorrow is your wedding day."

"It is, and I am happy. And I am so grateful for all you have done in preparation for a wonderful day."

"It is nothing."

"And I am so overjoyed to be free from slavery and permitted to marry Regulus. One day, I hope to be a citizen of Rome."

"I am here to help make that happen. We women must do what we can for each other in a world of men and their brutal actions."

"Not all men are like that. Regulus is kind and gentle."

"True, but beware the men that wield power and influence. They make life hell for people like us when they write laws to suit their own inclinations and selfish ambitions."

"Do you think there will be any justice in this world?"

"Some, but it's hard to find and even harder to access for so many that don't know their way around the courts – you should come inside now and warm yourself by the fire."

"I will – no doubt Dido is wondering where I am."

"Ah, yes, she has grown quite attached to you."

Regulus and Sabina's wedding day arrived under a blue dome of sunlit spring. The *Belisama Cygnus* rowers had erected an improvised gazebo, four oars planted in the ground next to the river above the loading dock with the boat's red sail draped over to provide cover for the bride, groom, bridesmaids, and the priest. The village and the fort hummed with expectation. Everyone loved a good wedding not least of all for the feast that came with one, and that was especially true after the rationing, which had come into force since victory over Festus and his rebel army. Lyra had been generous to a fault ensuring supplies of food and wine had been shipped into Bremetenn in time for the wedding feast. Now was to be a time of celebration and plenty.

Regulus had made multiple trips on the river right up until the day before the wedding and, at Lyra's request, he had brought Sabina's two slave friends up from Portus Piscium, ostensibly to serve guests at the feast. They had escaped the death penalty since it could not be proved that Festus owned them legally, all things pointing to the possibility that they, like Sabina, had been stolen in the first place. Lyra was working on getting them freed by manumission along with Astrid so she could be with Marcellus.

Sabina had sent word to Deva for Evander to come and give her his blessing, and she was pleased to hear he was in Bremetenn. Despite the fact that she had been his slave, she still regarded him as her father figure. He was, after all, the only one she had ever known, and although he had given his blessing to Regulus and her in private, his being present at the ceremony would add to the official side of things in keeping with Roman marriage traditions.

Lyra was most particular about everything, not least of all the bride and bridesmaids. Everything had to be just so, including her own white toga. Seren, Lyra, and two young girls from the village would be in train behind Sabina when they walked over to the gazebo. Sabina had pleaded for Astrid and the two slave girls from Portus Piscium to be bridesmaids, but Decimus would have none of it. They were slaves, and therefore, not allowed.

When the hour arrived for the bride and bridesmaids to make their way to the river from Lyra's apartment, Lyra went outside to check the shadow on the sundial. Satisfied that it was time, she urged them all to come forward. The bridal party walked at a stately pace to the gazebo and assembled before a priest. Sabina stood in her ankle length white robe with an orange shawl that draped over her head down to her waist. A white cord that wound around her waist was tied with the Knot of Hercules, which only the groom was allowed to untie.

Further up the road through the village, Regulus led a procession of all the villagers in Bremetenn from Seren's apartment down towards the gazebo. All the soldiers came out of the fort to watch. Decimus came out of the fort to join the procession alongside Seren, which pleased Regulus. Evander plodded along as best as his failing legs would allow.

The procession arrived at the gazebo and Regulus took his place facing Sabina in front of the priest. Seren had made him a white linen tunic edged with red bands around the bottom hem, wrists, and neck. His hair was cropped short and, freshly bathed, he and Sabina looked every inch a Roman couple starting out on married life. Both had flirted with death and triumphed over the odds.

The crowd stood in reverent silence as the priest offered prayers and invocations to the gods for fortune to favour the couple before him. Then he announced that it was time for Regulus and Sabina to join hands as they faced each other.

"Where you are, I am too," said Regulus.

"Where you are, I am too," replied Sabina.

They sealed their wedding vows with a kiss and the crowd erupted with cheers and applause. Soldiers cheered and clattered their swords from the fort, looking forward to joining the feast. Decimus had arranged for all of them to attend in shifts as groups were given leave from guard duty. Regulus and Sabina had insisted that everyone should have the opportunity to attend the celebrations at some point during the day. Two were now as one, all barriers to their union dispelled after one lunar cycle that started with a desperate escape and a thwarted ambush.

Long wooden tables laden with food and wine had been laid out next to the river: bread, venison, salmon, olives, lamb, pork, and even the cantankerous baker's special meat pies. The wine flowed and with it, the conversations and laughter grew louder. Astrid and the two slave girls managed a brief conversation, each counting the days until Lyra could complete all formalities and payment to secure their freedom. Regulus and Sabina were mobbed by well-wishers. Everyone was engaged in good-humoured conversation except Lyra who stood to one side beaming with benevolence at the scene, remembering how the expense of the feast had been afforded by the "acquisition" of Festus Crassus's ill-gotten fortune.

She remembered that night when Bremetenn was full of soldiers of the Legio XX. She remembered how she had slipped out of her apartment and how little time it taken her to find an attractive woman plying her stock in trade and pay her to seduce and drug the prison guard. And how she had paid the two burly slaves at the bath house furnace room to carry the chest out from the prison to the woods and bury it, and to wait until she called them to bring it to her. She had known all along that Sextus had made her the sole beneficiary in his will. The only thing that Lyra had not planned for was Sextus's death. That was an unforeseen happenstance that popped the cherry on the cake.

Satisfied that everything was in place, she decided to join in and socialise with the wedding guests, each expressing their gratitude for such a wonderful feast.

Then she froze, open-mouthed in disbelief. A tall trim elderly man in a smart white toga with white hair cropped short and a Mediterranean tan was walking towards her with two young slave women walking in attendance behind hm. As he drew closer, he called out to her.

"Salva Lyra, how goes your day?"

"Marius?"

Belisama, the ancient goddess of the sun, moon, and fire in Britannia babbled and sang her stories through the river that the Romans had named after her. Stories that flowed down through the never-ending echoes of time and stories of things yet to come as the sun and moon chased each other across the sky. Stories we can still hear if we would but stop and listen.